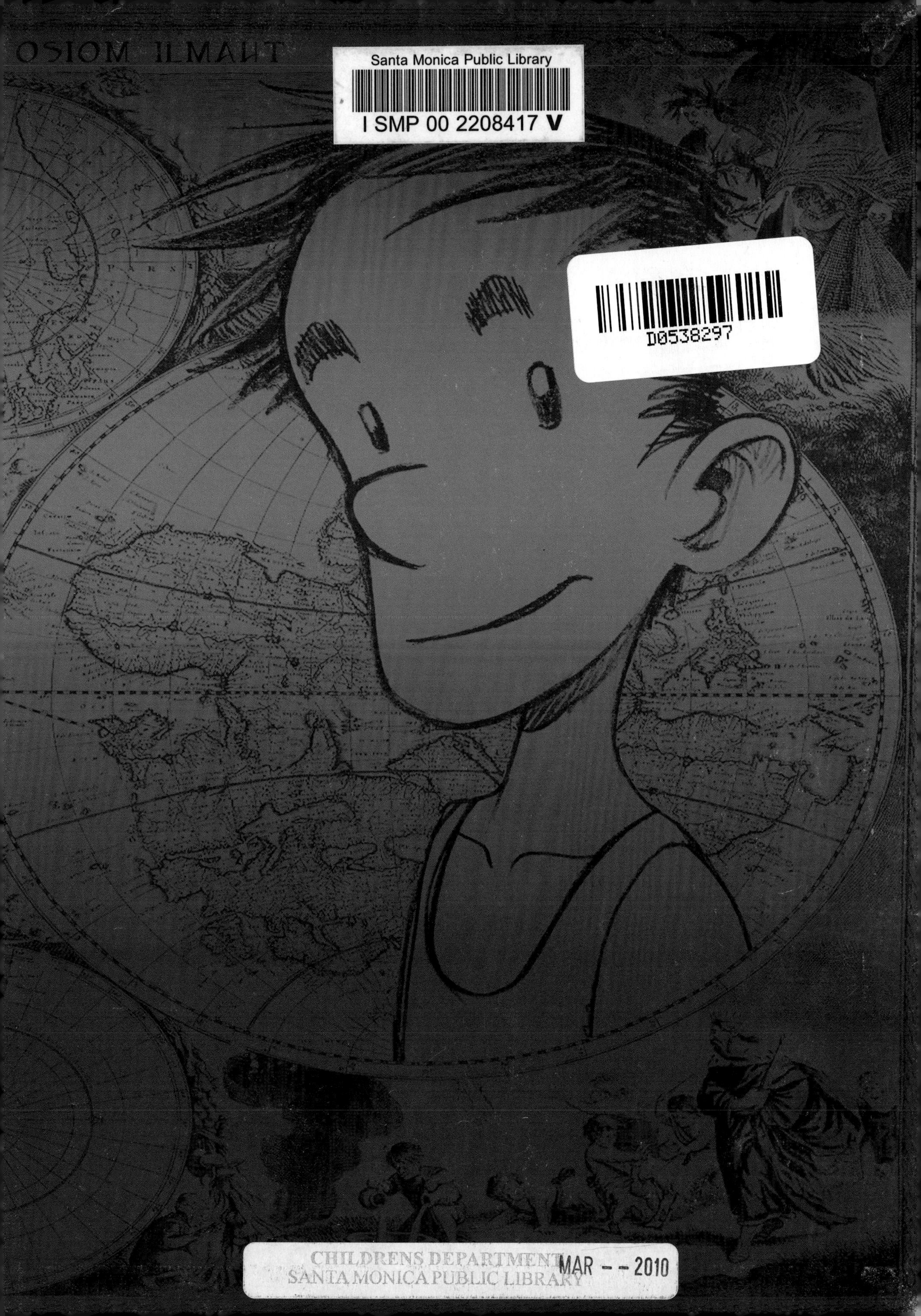

the ElseWheRe CHRONICLES

BOOK ONE
THE SHADOW DOOR

AR+
BANNISTER

S+ORY
NYKKO

COLORS
JAFFRÉ

GRAPHIC UNIVERSE™ • MINNEAPOLIS • NEW YORK

To Sabine, Léo, and Noé

—Nykko

For Flora, thank you for your
psychological and culinary support.
—Bannister

To Mathilde
—Jaffré

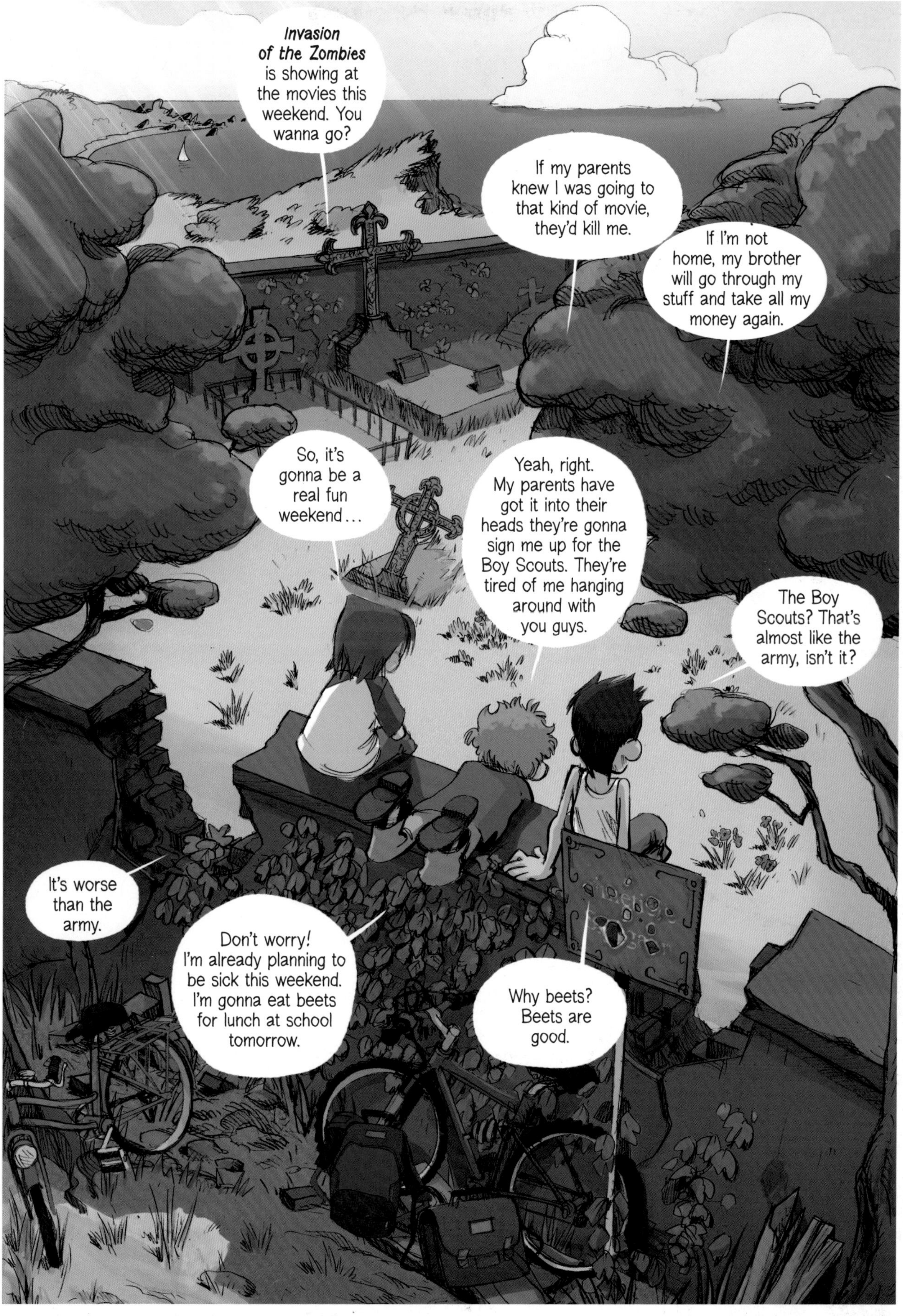
Invasion of the Zombies is showing at the movies this weekend. You wanna go?
If my parents knew I was going to that kind of movie, they'd kill me.
If I'm not home, my brother will go through my stuff and take all my money again.
So, it's gonna be a real fun weekend...
Yeah, right. My parents have got it into their heads they're gonna sign me up for the Boy Scouts. They're tired of me hanging around with you guys.
The Boy Scouts? That's almost like the army, isn't it?
It's worse than the army.
Don't worry! I'm already planning to be sick this weekend. I'm gonna eat beets for lunch at school tomorrow.
Why beets? Beets are good.

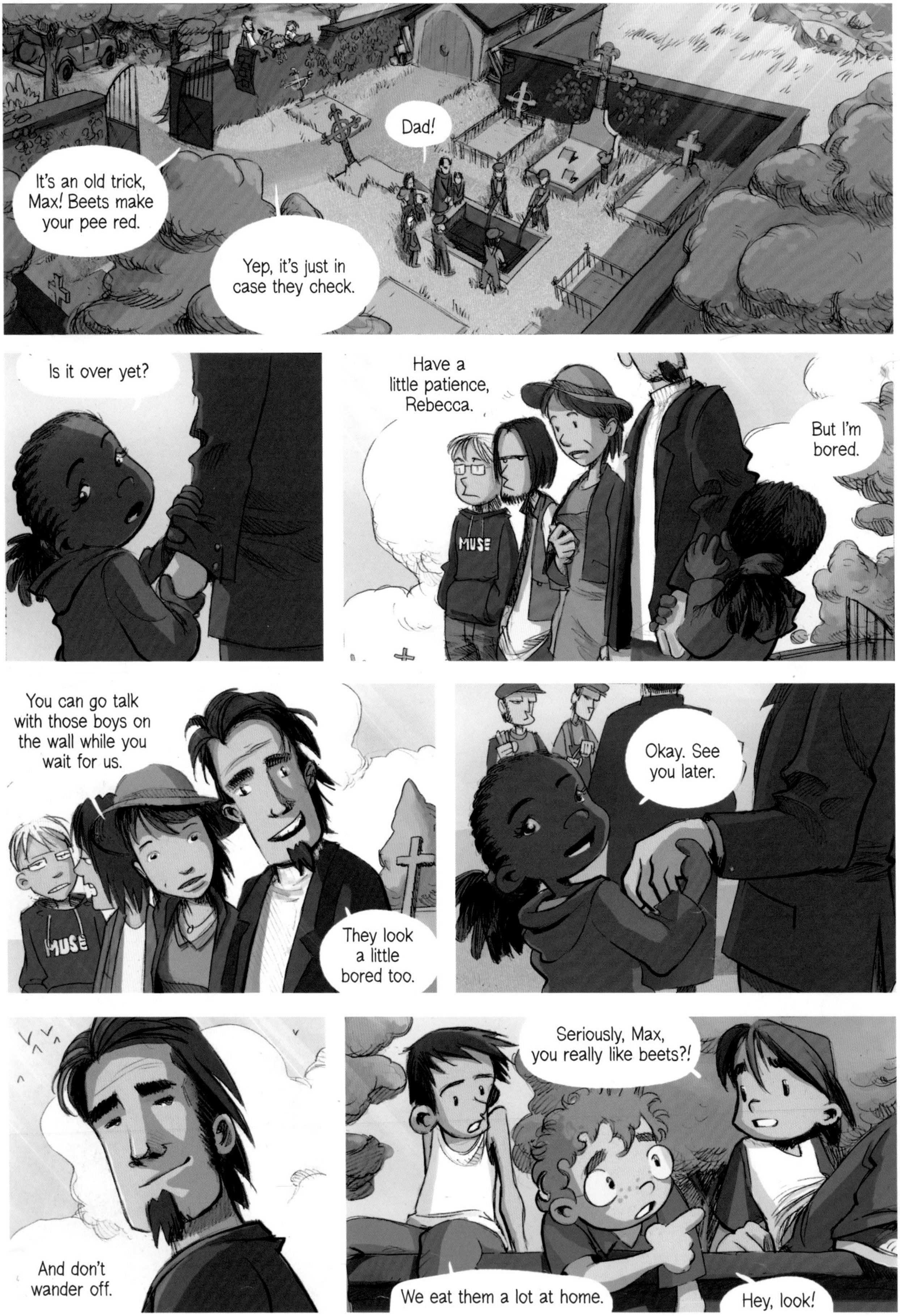
Dad!
It's an old trick, Max! Beets make your pee red.
Yep, it's just in case they check.
Is it over yet?
Have a little patience, Rebecca.
But I'm bored.
You can go talk with those boys on the wall while you wait for us.
They look a little bored too.
Okay. See you later.
And don't wander off.
Seriously, Max, you really like beets?!
We eat them a lot at home.
Hey, look!

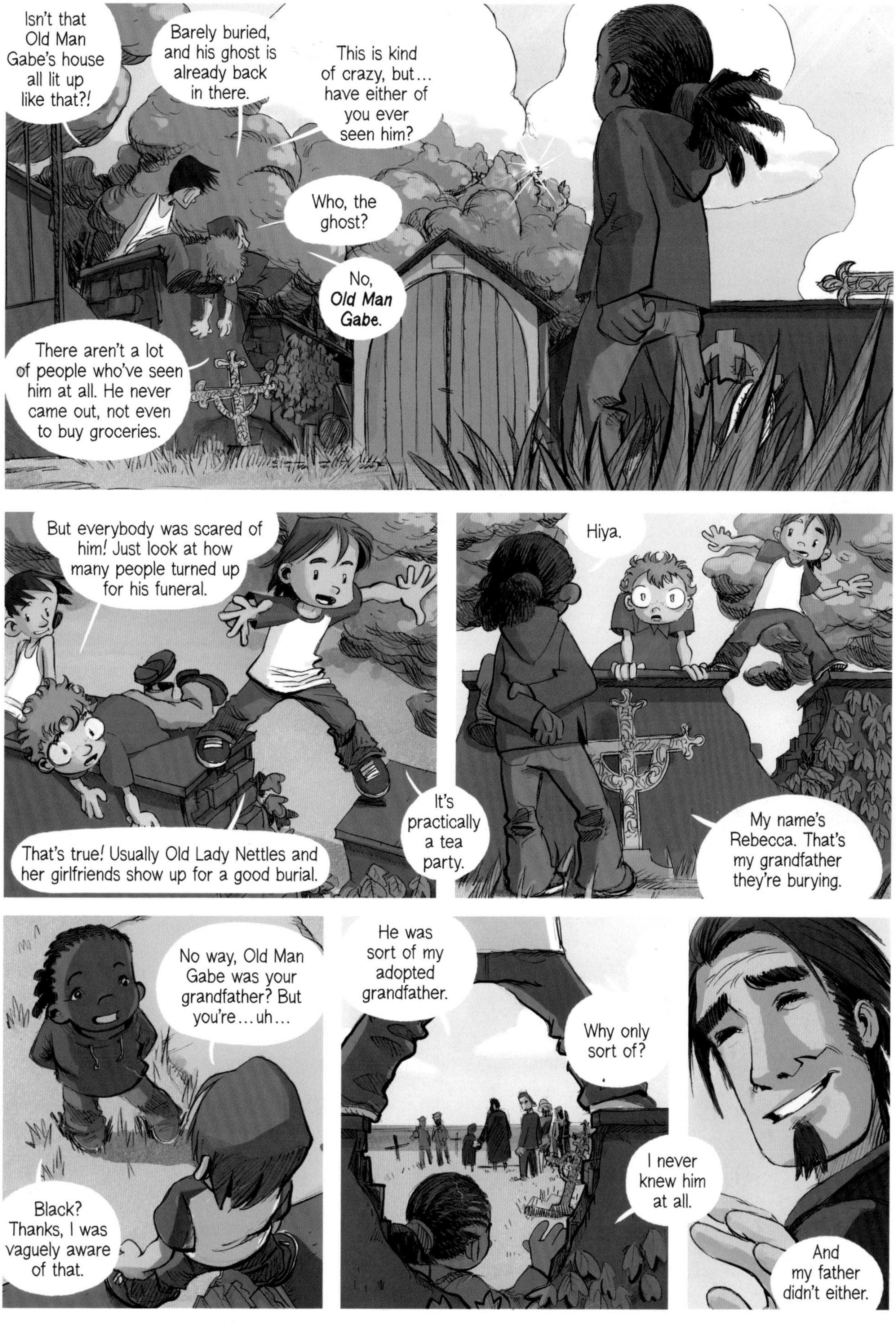
Isn't that Old Man Gabe's house all lit up like that?!
Barely buried, and his ghost is already back in there.
This is kind of crazy, but... have either of you ever seen him?
Who, the ghost?
No, Old Man Gabe.
There aren't a lot of people who've seen him at all. He never came out, not even to buy groceries.
But everybody was scared of him! Just look at how many people turned up for his funeral.
That's true! Usually Old Lady Nettles and her girlfriends show up for a good burial.
It's practically a tea party.
Hiya.
My name's Rebecca. That's my grandfather they're burying.
No way, Old Man Gabe was your grandfather? But you're...uh...
Black? Thanks, I was vaguely aware of that.
He was sort of my adopted grandfather.
Why only sort of?
I never knew him at all.
And my father didn't either.

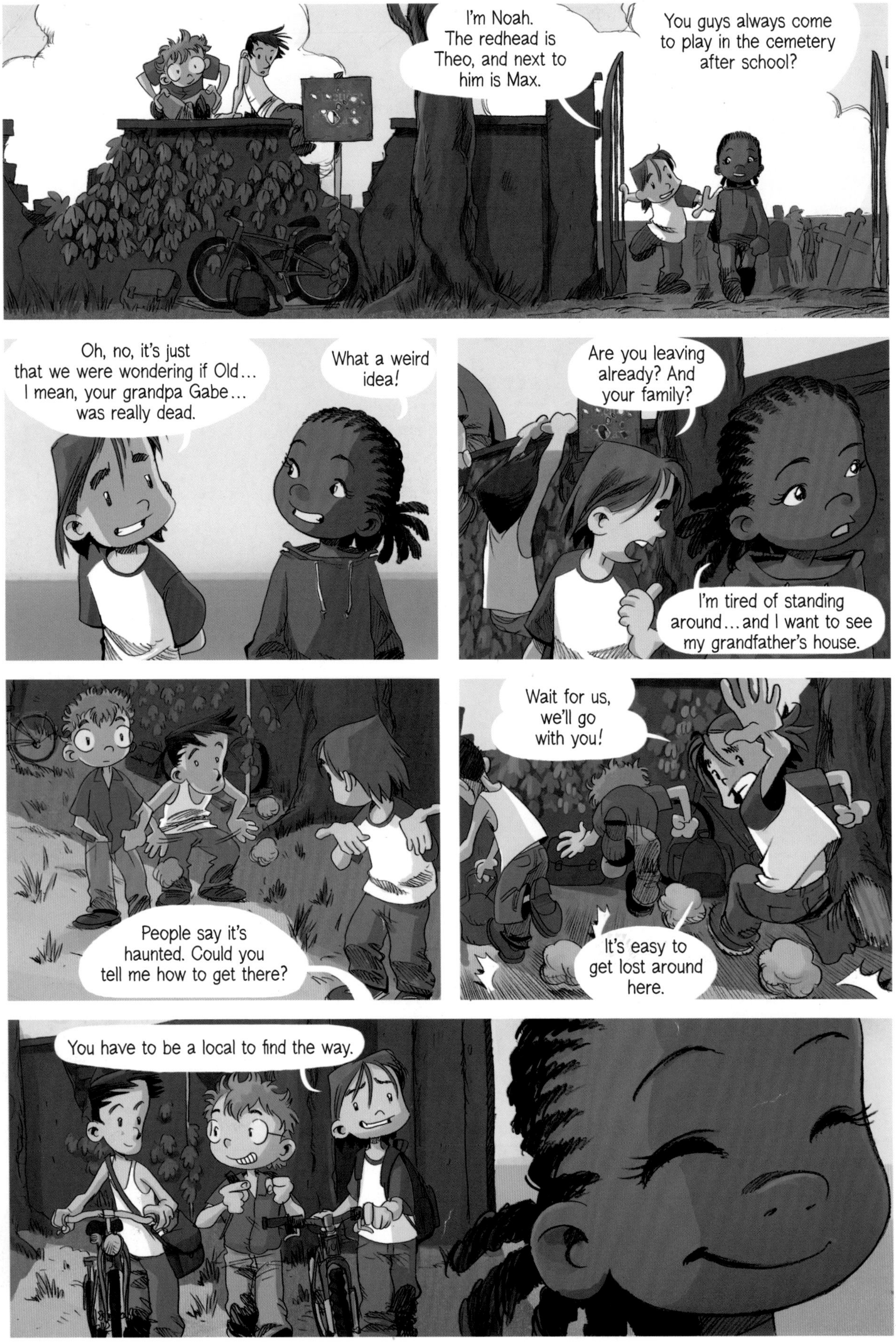

I'm Noah. The redhead is Theo, and next to him is Max.
You guys always come to play in the cemetery after school?
Oh, no, it's just that we were wondering if Old... I mean, your grandpa Gabe... was really dead.
What a weird idea!
Are you leaving already? And your family?
I'm tired of standing around... and I want to see my grandfather's house.
People say it's haunted. Could you tell me how to get there?
Wait for us, we'll go with you!
It's easy to get lost around here.
You have to be a local to find the way.

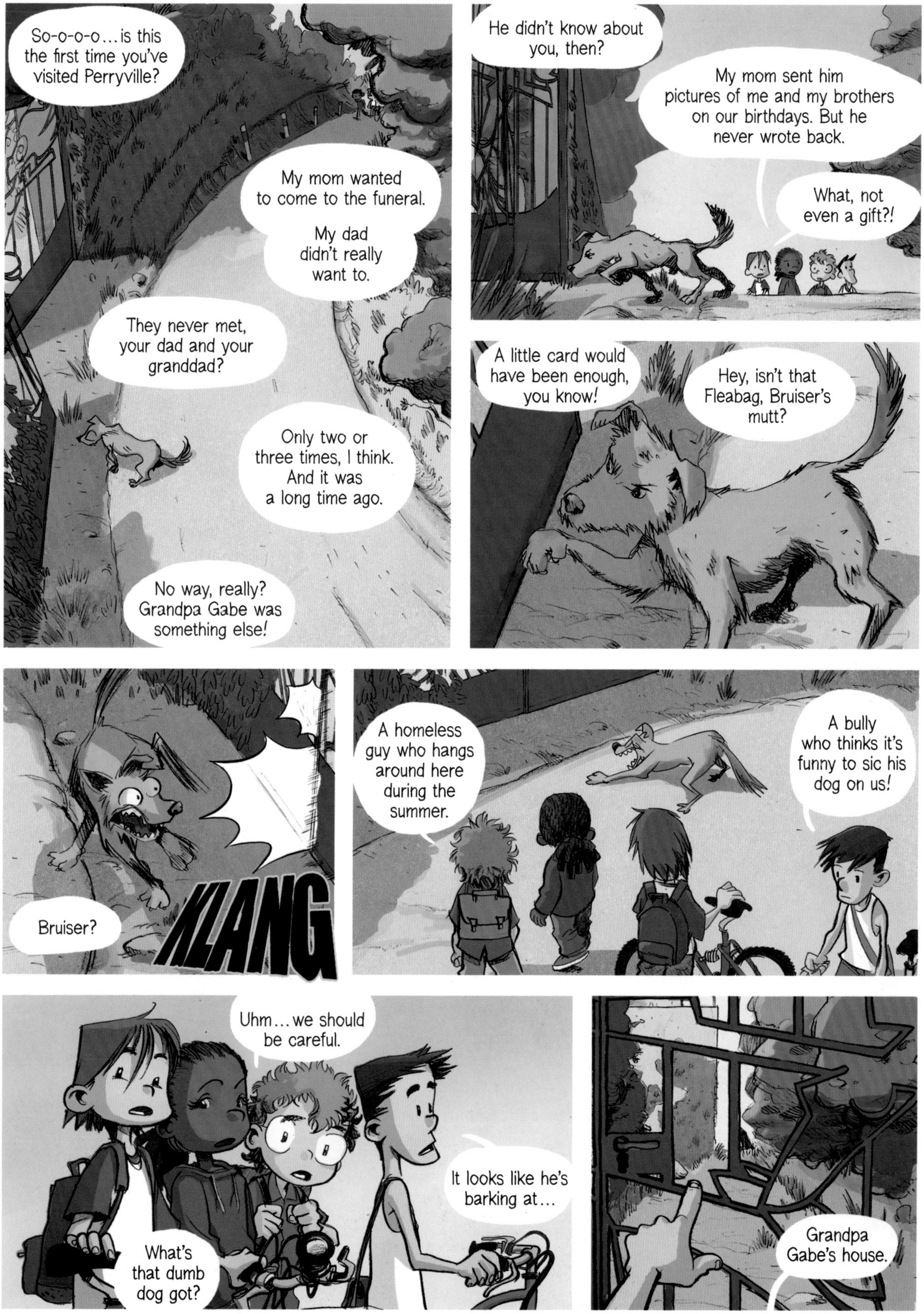

So-o-o-o...is this the first time you've visited Perryville?
My mom wanted to come to the funeral.
My dad didn't really want to.
They never met, your dad and your granddad?
Only two or three times, I think. And it was a long time ago.
No way, really? Grandpa Gabe was something else!
He didn't know about you, then?
My mom sent him pictures of me and my brothers on our birthdays. But he never wrote back.
What, not even a gift?!
A little card would have been enough, you know!
Hey, isn't that Fleabag, Bruiser's mutt?
Bruiser?
KLANG
A homeless guy who hangs around here during the summer.
A bully who thinks it's funny to sic his dog on us!
Uhm...we should be careful.
What's that dumb dog got?
It looks like he's barking at...
Grandpa Gabe's house.

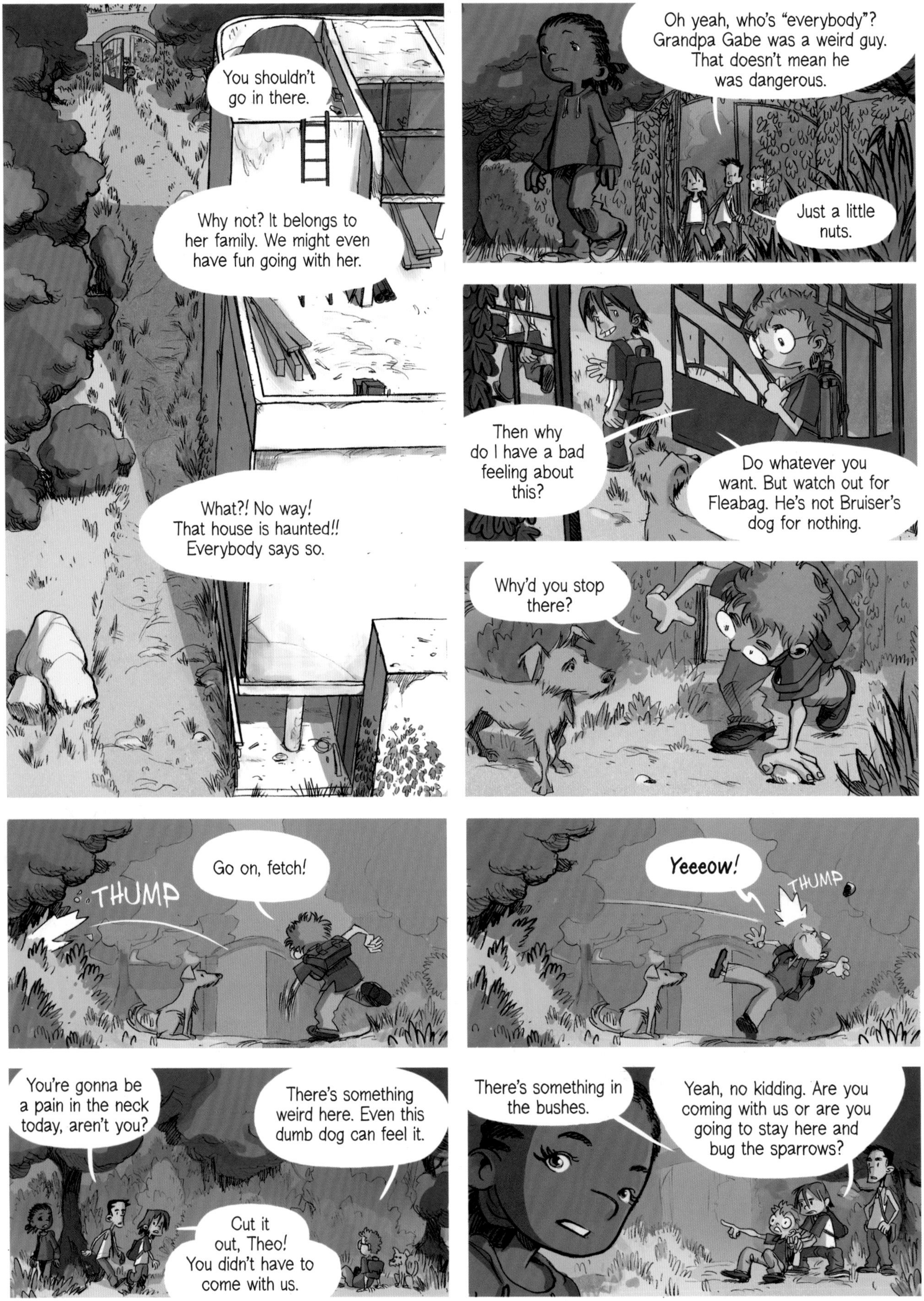
You shouldn't go in there.
Why not? It belongs to her family. We might even have fun going with her.
What?! No way! That house is haunted!! Everybody says so.
Oh yeah, who's "everybody"? Grandpa Gabe was a weird guy. That doesn't mean he was dangerous.
Just a little nuts.
Then why do I have a bad feeling about this?
Do whatever you want. But watch out for Fleabag. He's not Bruiser's dog for nothing.
Why'd you stop there?
Go on, fetch!
THUMP
Yeeeow!
THUMP
You're gonna be a pain in the neck today, aren't you?
There's something weird here. Even this dumb dog can feel it.
Cut it out, Theo! You didn't have to come with us.
There's something in the bushes.
Yeah, no kidding. Are you coming with us or are you going to stay here and bug the sparrows?

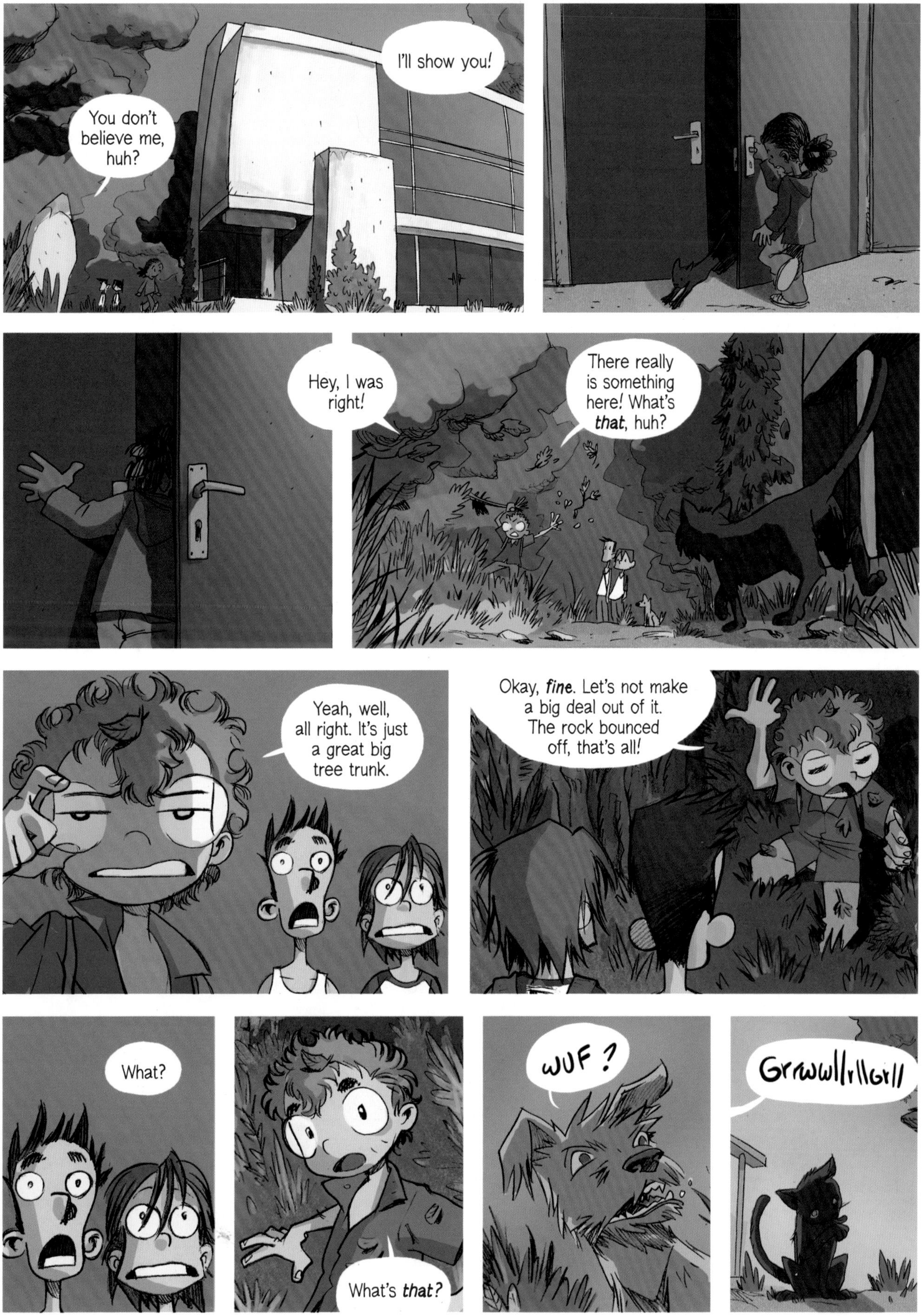
You don't believe me, huh?
I'll show you!
Hey, I was right!
There really is something here! What's *that*, huh?
Yeah, well, all right. It's just a great big tree trunk.
Okay, *fine*. Let's not make a big deal out of it. The rock bounced off, that's all!
What?
What's *that?*
WUF ?
Grrwwllrllgrll

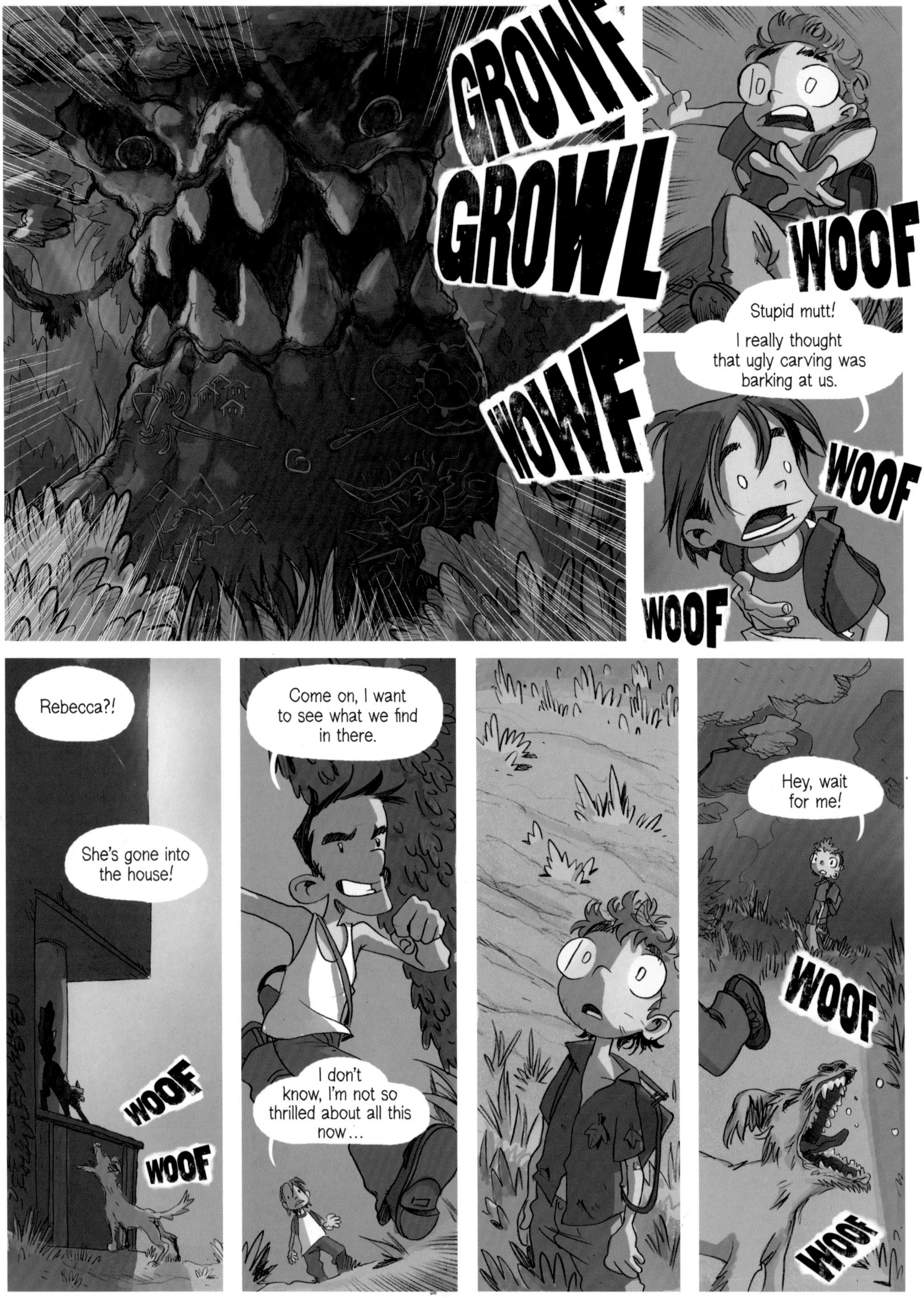
GROWF
GROWL
WOWF
WOOF
Stupid mutt!
I really thought that ugly carving was barking at us.
WOOF
WOOF
Rebecca?!
She's gone into the house!
WOOF
WOOF
Come on, I want to see what we find in there.
I don't know, I'm not so thrilled about all this now...
Hey, wait for me!
WOOF
WOOF

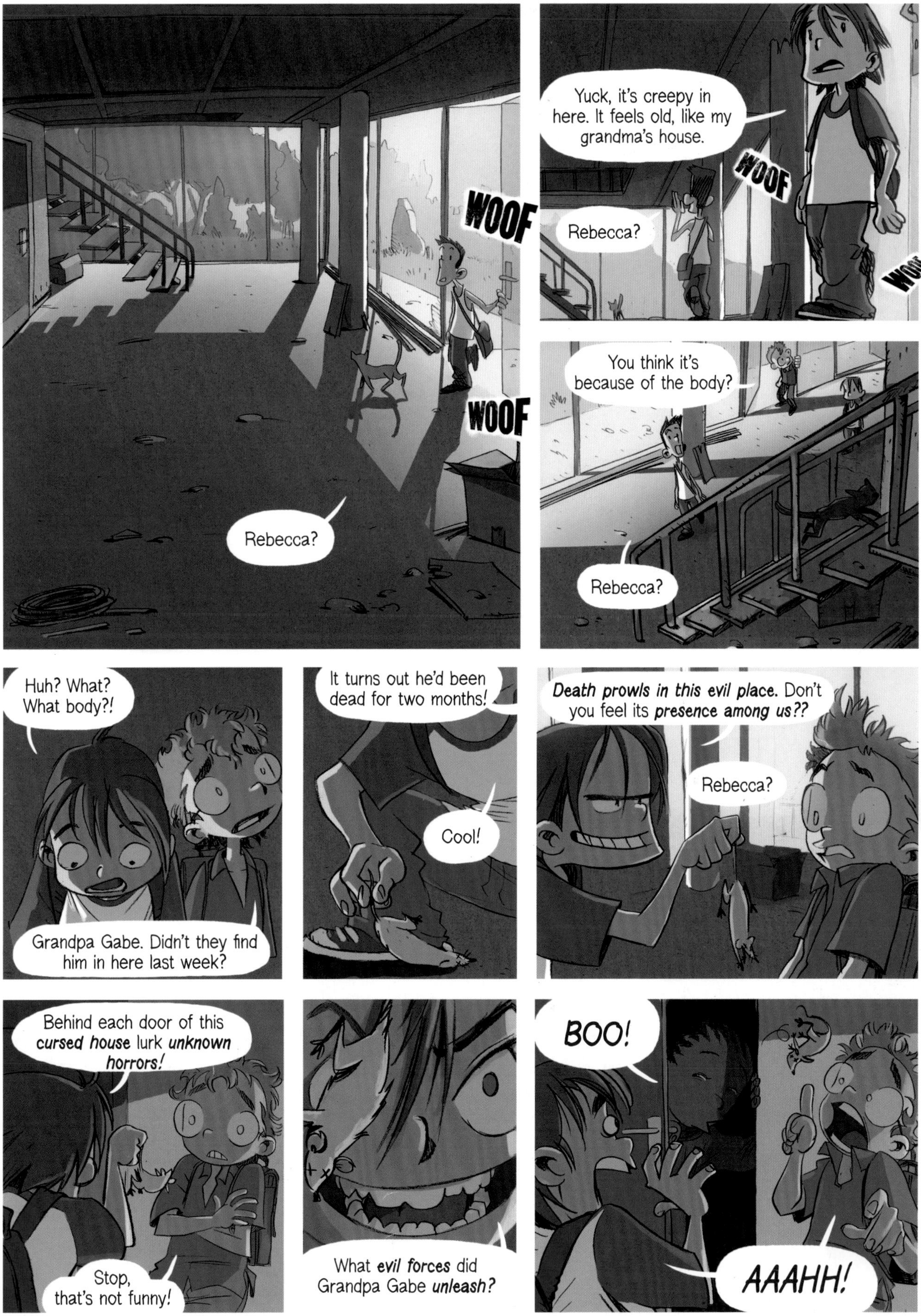
WOOF
WOOF
Rebecca?
Yuck, it's creepy in here. It feels old, like my grandma's house.
WOOF
Rebecca?
WOOF
You think it's because of the body?
Rebecca?
Huh? What? What body?!
Grandpa Gabe. Didn't they find him in here last week?
It turns out he'd been dead for two months!
Cool!
Death prowls in this evil place. Don't you feel its ***presence among us??***
Rebecca?
Behind each door of this ***cursed house*** lurk ***unknown horrors!***
Stop, that's not funny!
What ***evil forces*** did Grandpa Gabe ***unleash?***
BOO!
AAAHH!

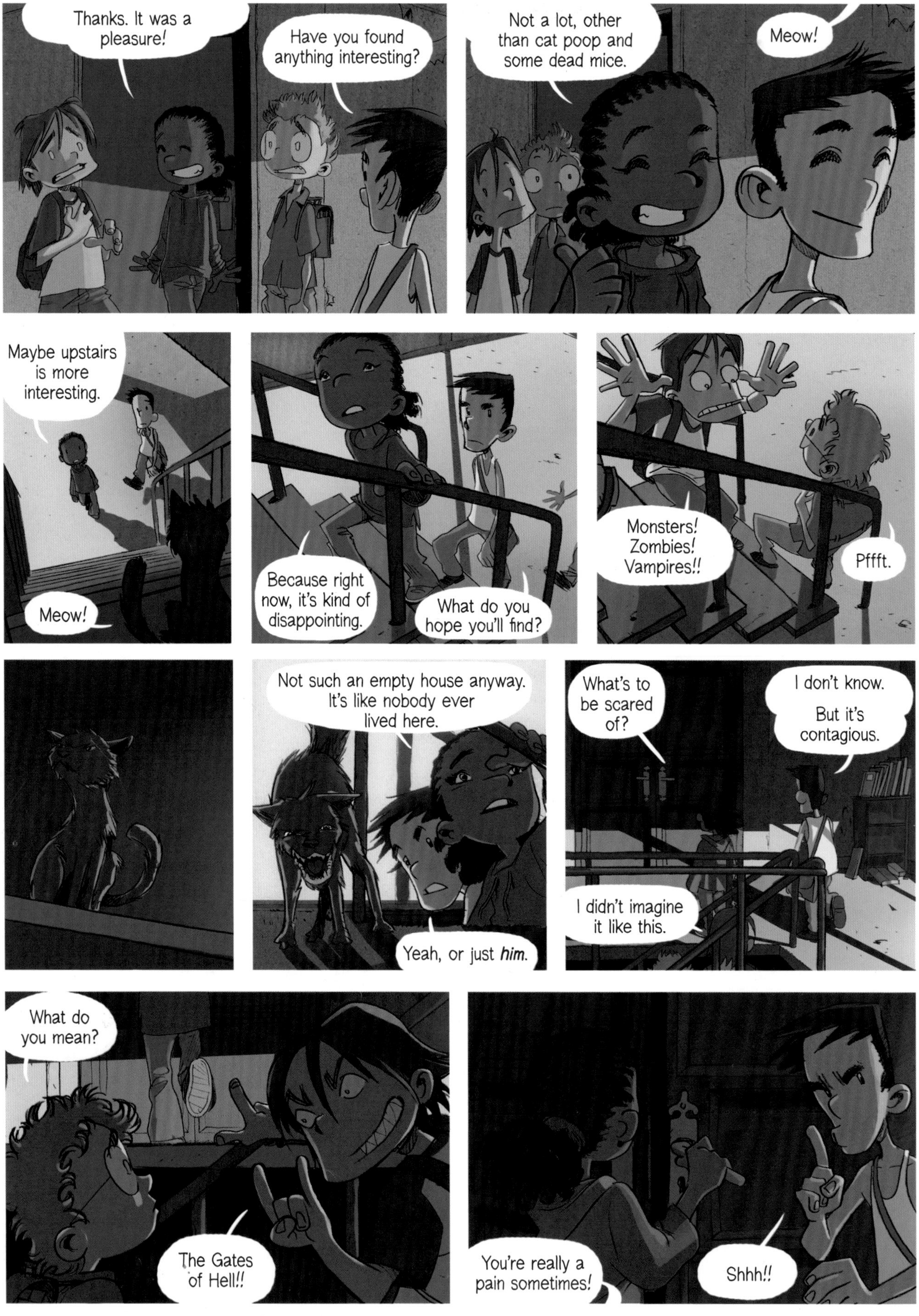
Thanks. It was a pleasure!
Have you found anything interesting?
Not a lot, other than cat poop and some dead mice.
Meow!
Maybe upstairs is more interesting.
Meow!
Because right now, it's kind of disappointing.
What do you hope you'll find?
Monsters! Zombies! Vampires!!
Pffft.
Not such an empty house anyway. It's like nobody ever lived here.
Yeah, or just *him*.
What's to be scared of?
I don't know.
But it's contagious.
I didn't imagine it like this.
What do you mean?
The Gates of Hell!!
You're really a pain sometimes!
Shhh!!

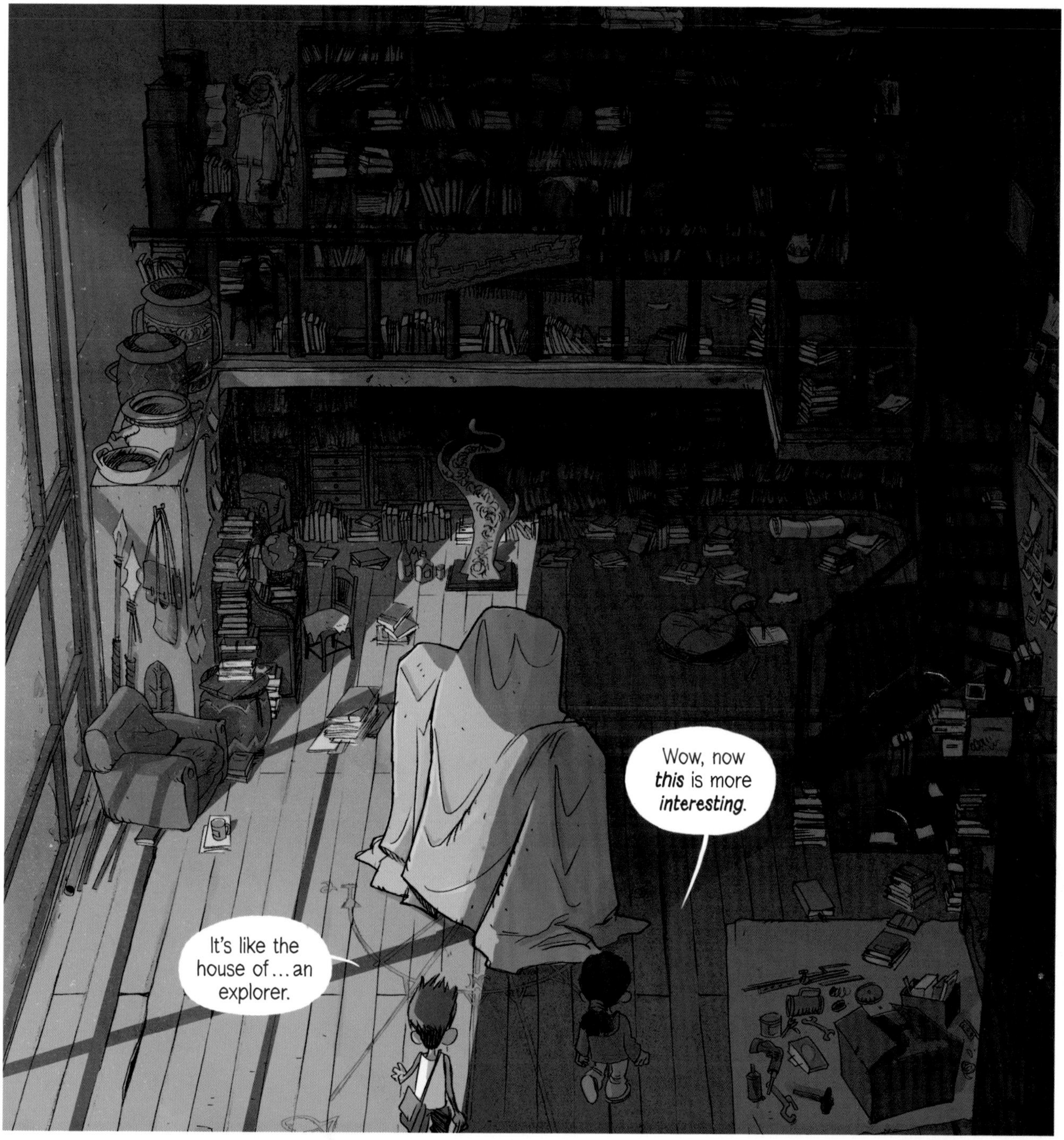
Wow, now *this* is more *interesting*.
It's like the house of... an explorer.

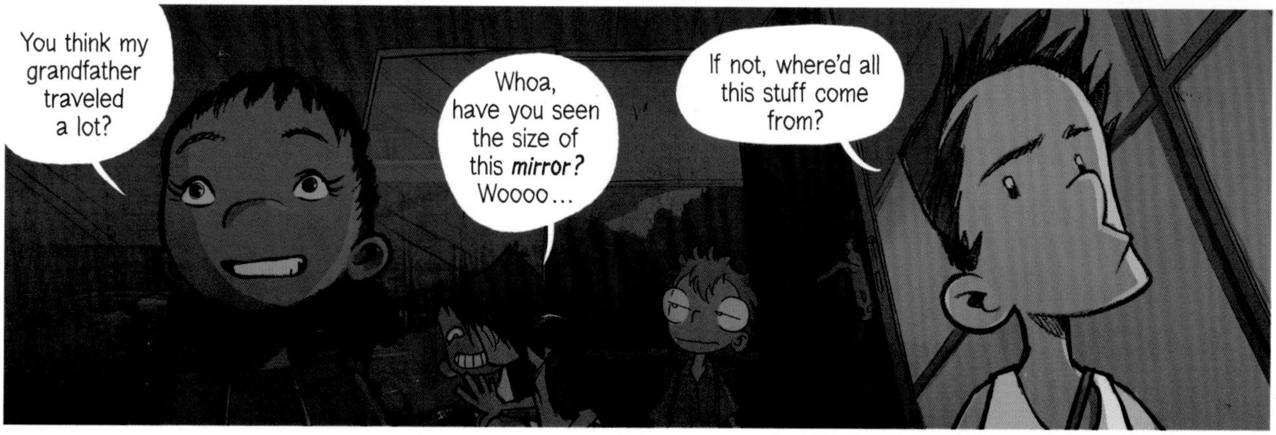
You think my grandfather traveled a lot?
Whoa, have you seen the size of this *mirror?* Woooo...
If not, where'd all this stuff come from?

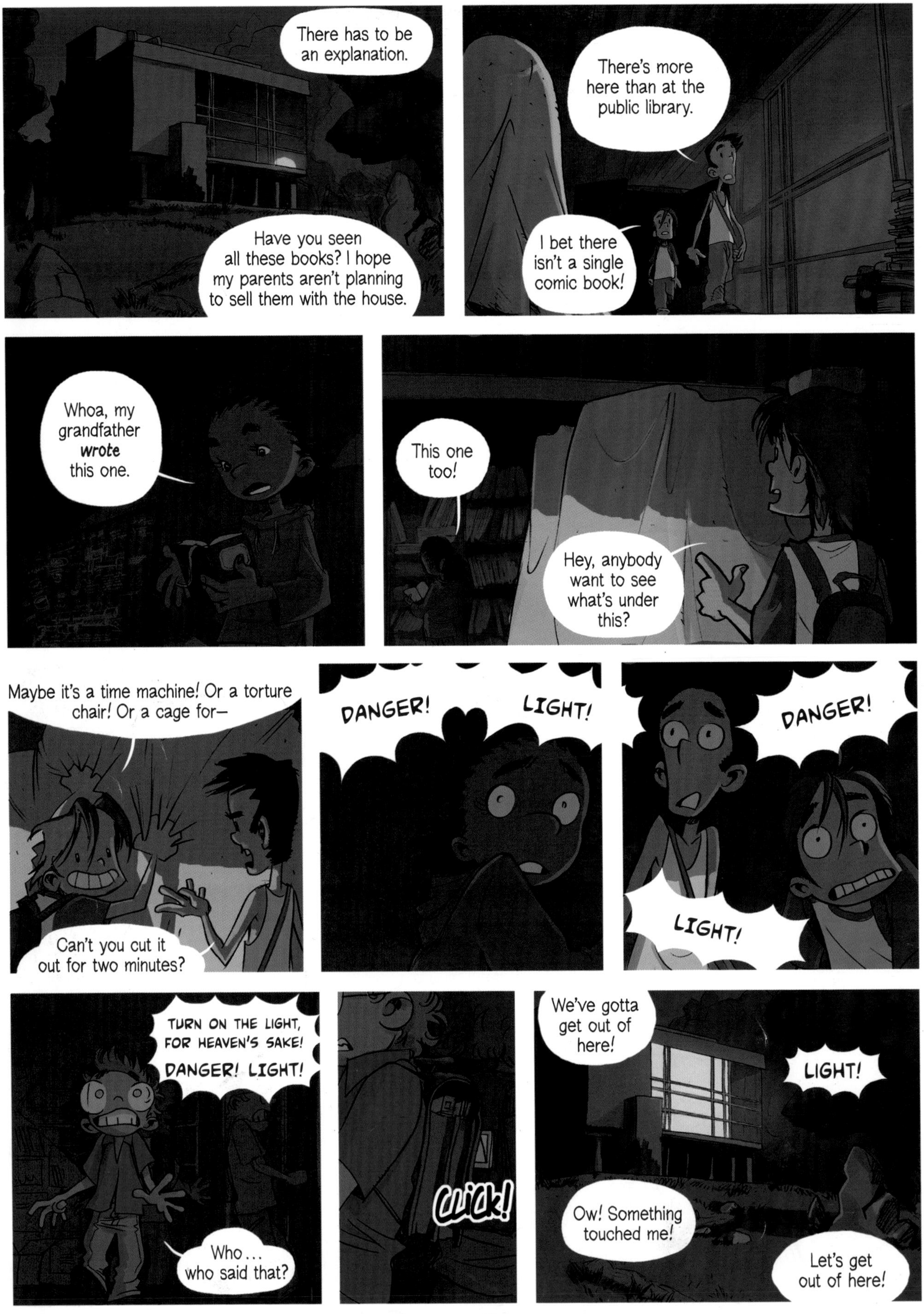
There has to be an explanation.
Have you seen all these books? I hope my parents aren't planning to sell them with the house.
There's more here than at the public library.
I bet there isn't a single comic book!
Whoa, my grandfather **wrote** this one.
This one too!
Hey, anybody want to see what's under this?
Maybe it's a time machine! Or a torture chair! Or a cage for—
Can't you cut it out for two minutes?
DANGER!
LIGHT!
DANGER!
LIGHT!
TURN ON THE LIGHT, FOR HEAVEN'S SAKE!
DANGER! LIGHT!
Who... who said that?
CLICK!
We've gotta get out of here!
LIGHT!
Ow! Something touched me!
Let's get out of here!

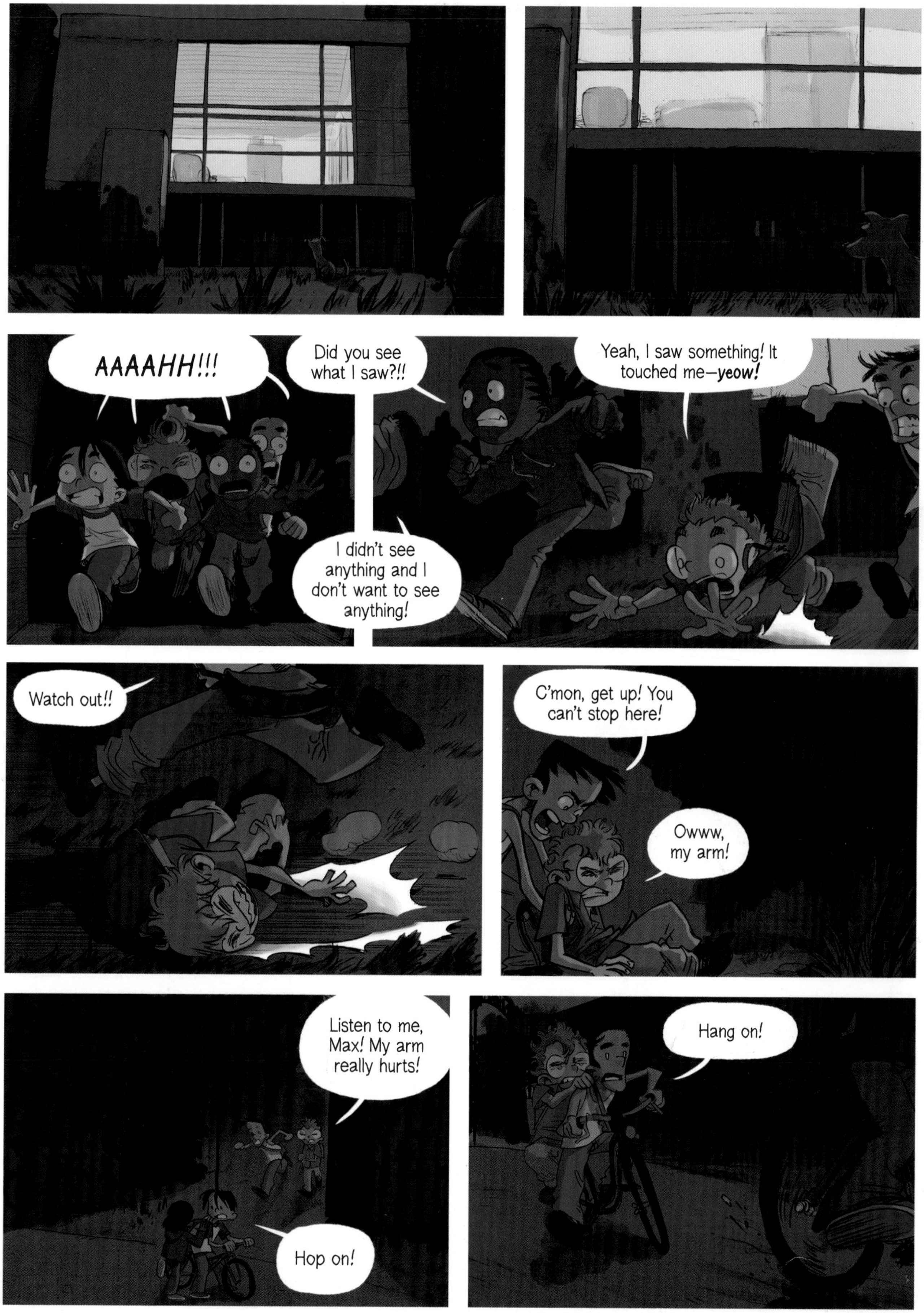
AAAAHH!!!
Did you see what I saw?!!
I didn't see anything and I don't want to see anything!
Yeah, I saw something! It touched me—*yeow!*
Watch out!!
C'mon, get up! You can't stop here!
Owww, my arm!
Listen to me, Max! My arm really hurts!
Hop on!
Hang on!

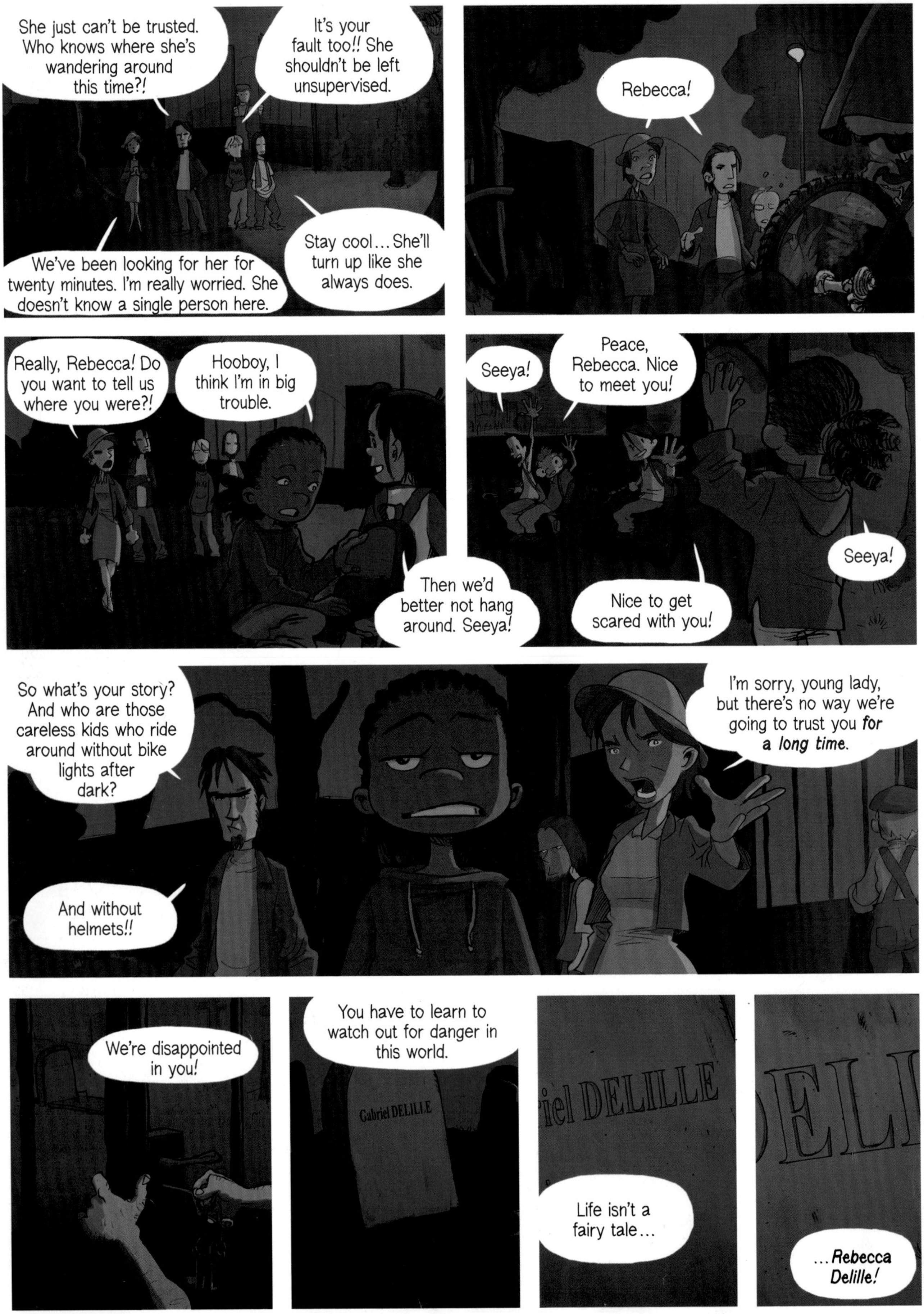
She just can't be trusted. Who knows where she's wandering around this time?!
It's your fault too!! She shouldn't be left unsupervised.
We've been looking for her for twenty minutes. I'm really worried. She doesn't know a single person here.
Stay cool... She'll turn up like she always does.
Rebecca!
Really, Rebecca! Do you want to tell us where you were?!
Hooboy, I think I'm in big trouble.
Then we'd better not hang around. Seeya!
Seeya!
Peace, Rebecca. Nice to meet you!
Nice to get scared with you!
Seeya!
So what's your story? And who are those careless kids who ride around without bike lights after dark?
And without helmets!!
I'm sorry, young lady, but there's no way we're going to trust you ***for a long time***.
We're disappointed in you!
You have to learn to watch out for danger in this world.
Gabriel DELILLE
Life isn't a fairy tale...
riel DELILLE
...***Rebecca Delille!***

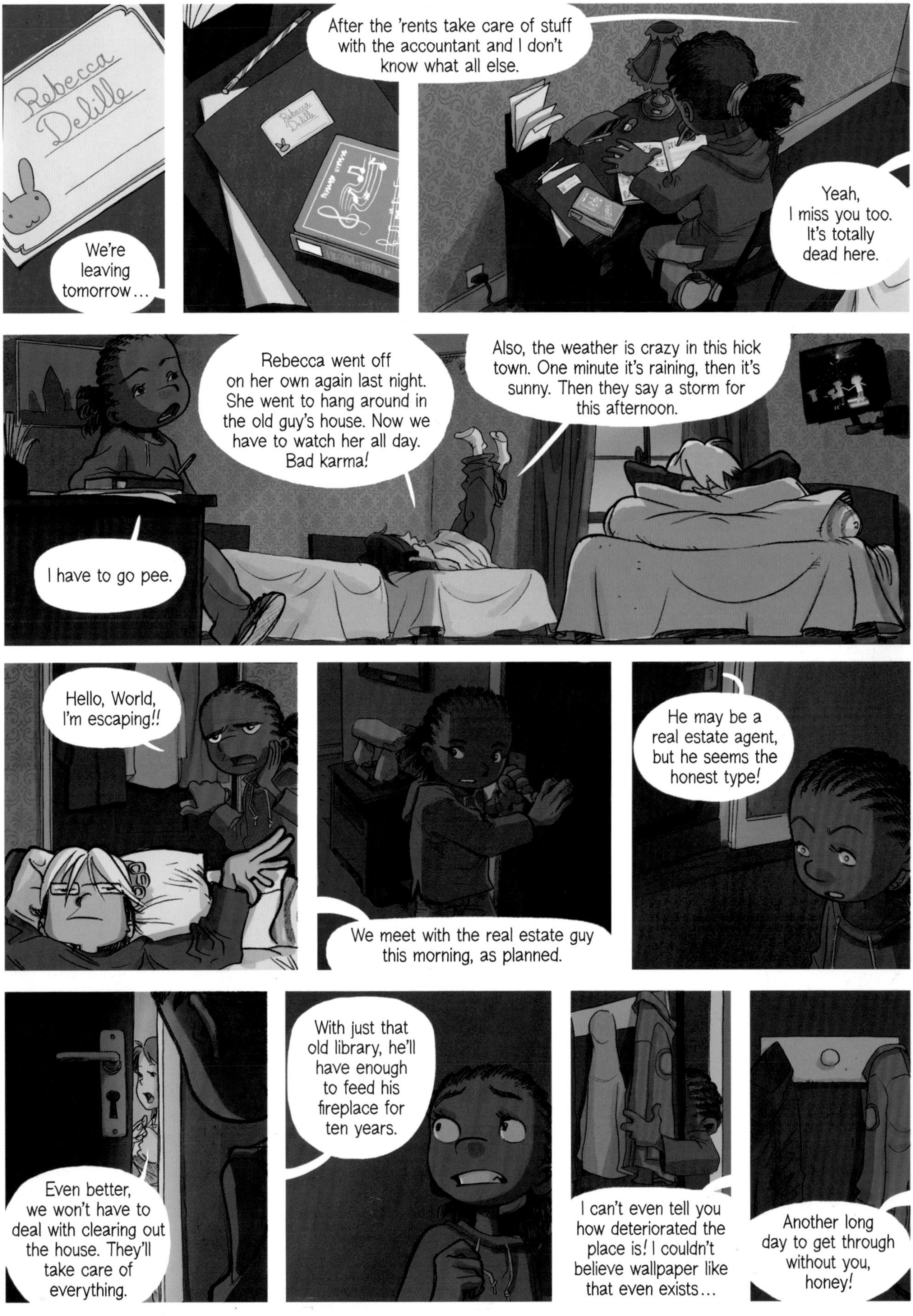
Rebecca Delille
We're leaving tomorrow…
After the 'rents take care of stuff with the accountant and I don't know what all else.
Yeah, I miss you too. It's totally dead here.
Rebecca went off on her own again last night. She went to hang around in the old guy's house. Now we have to watch her all day. Bad karma!
Also, the weather is crazy in this hick town. One minute it's raining, then it's sunny. Then they say a storm for this afternoon.
I have to go pee.
Hello, World, I'm escaping!!
We meet with the real estate guy this morning, as planned.
He may be a real estate agent, but he seems the honest type!
Even better, we won't have to deal with clearing out the house. They'll take care of everything.
With just that old library, he'll have enough to feed his fireplace for ten years.
I can't even tell you how deteriorated the place is! I couldn't believe wallpaper like that even exists…
Another long day to get through without you, honey!

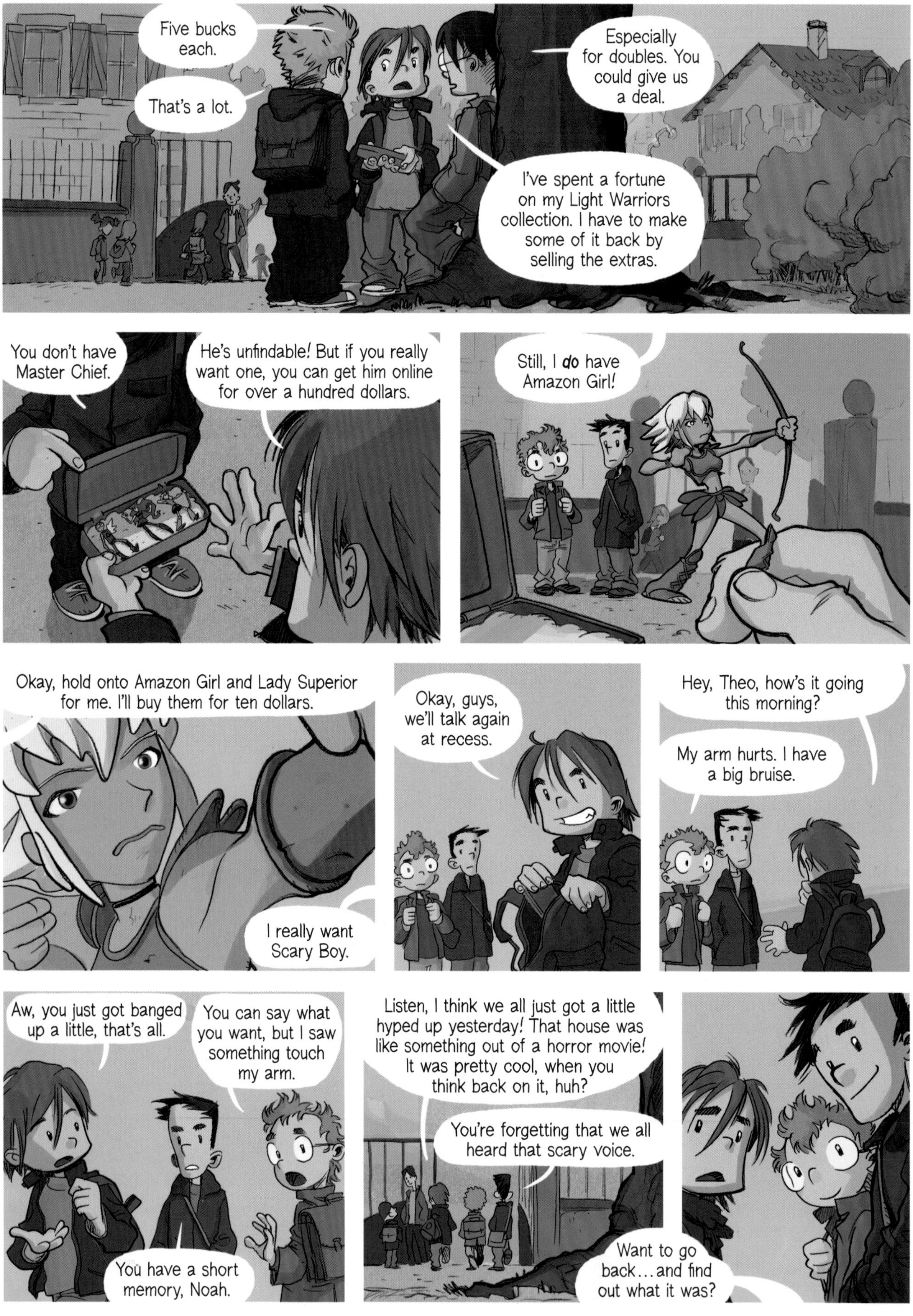
Five bucks each.
That's a lot.
Especially for doubles. You could give us a deal.
I've spent a fortune on my Light Warriors collection. I have to make some of it back by selling the extras.
You don't have Master Chief.
He's unfindable! But if you really want one, you can get him online for over a hundred dollars.
Still, I *do* have Amazon Girl!
Okay, hold onto Amazon Girl and Lady Superior for me. I'll buy them for ten dollars.
I really want Scary Boy.
Okay, guys, we'll talk again at recess.
Hey, Theo, how's it going this morning?
My arm hurts. I have a big bruise.
Aw, you just got banged up a little, that's all.
You can say what you want, but I saw something touch my arm.
You have a short memory, Noah.
Listen, I think we all just got a little hyped up yesterday! That house was like something out of a horror movie! It was pretty cool, when you think back on it, huh?
You're forgetting that we all heard that scary voice.
Want to go back... and find out what it was?

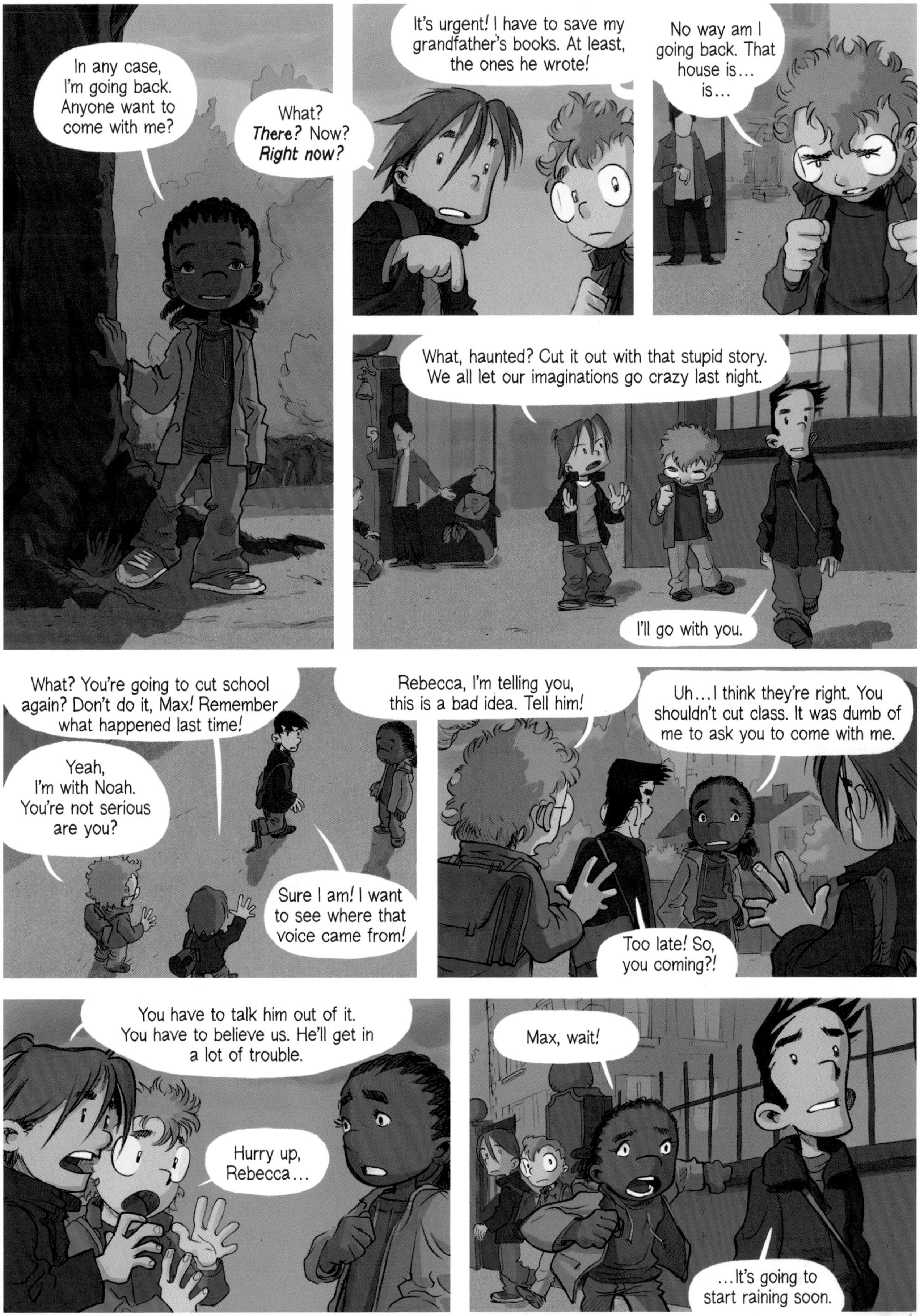
In any case, I'm going back. Anyone want to come with me?
What? *There?* Now? *Right now?*
It's urgent! I have to save my grandfather's books. At least, the ones he wrote!
No way am I going back. That house is... is...
What, haunted? Cut it out with that stupid story. We all let our imaginations go crazy last night.
I'll go with you.
What? You're going to cut school again? Don't do it, Max! Remember what happened last time!
Yeah, I'm with Noah. You're not serious are you?
Sure I am! I want to see where that voice came from!
Rebecca, I'm telling you, this is a bad idea. Tell him!
Uh...I think they're right. You shouldn't cut class. It was dumb of me to ask you to come with me.
Too late! So, you coming?!
You have to talk him out of it. You have to believe us. He'll get in a lot of trouble.
Hurry up, Rebecca...
Max, wait!
...It's going to start raining soon.

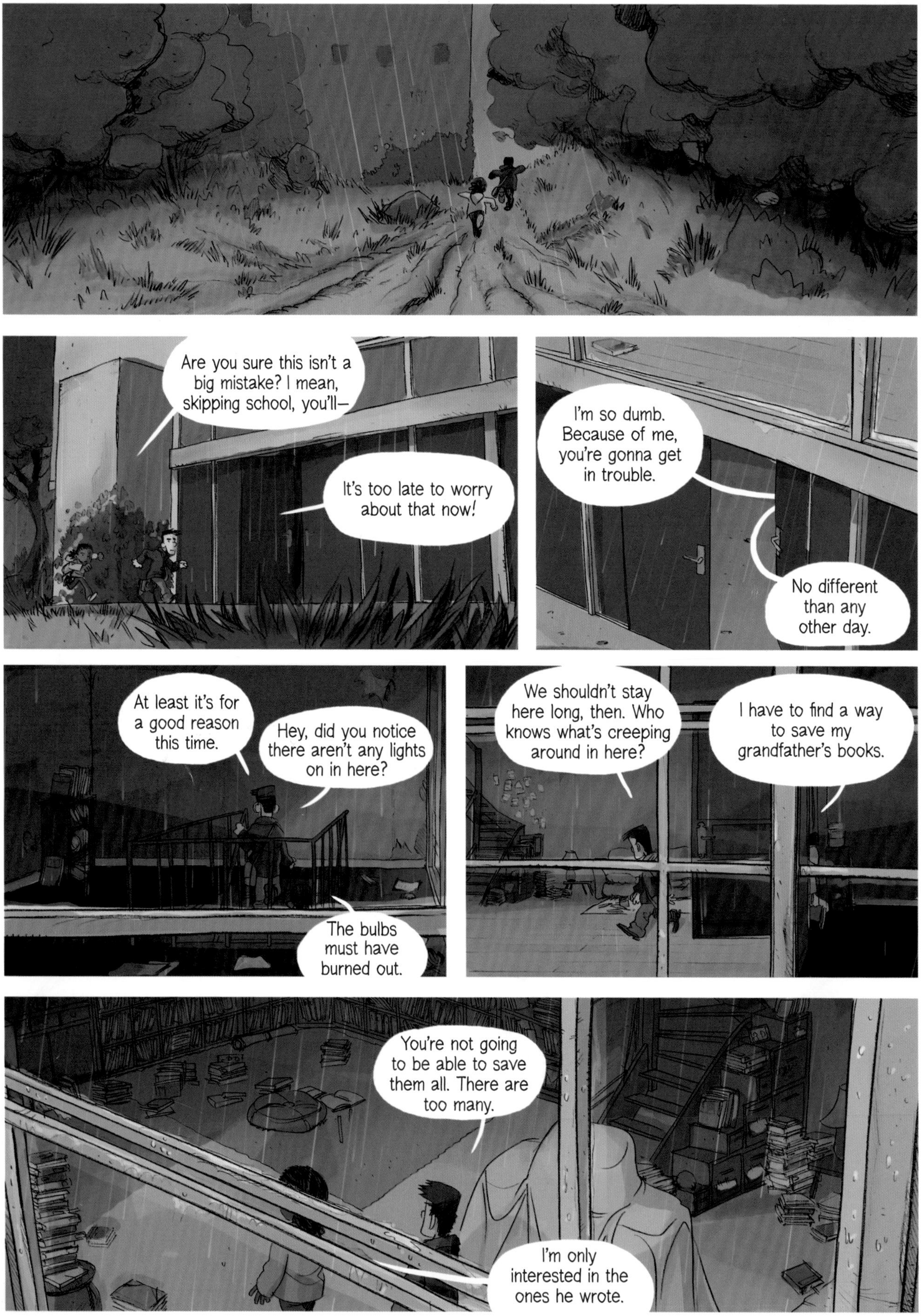
Are you sure this isn't a big mistake? I mean, skipping school, you'll–
It's too late to worry about that now!
I'm so dumb. Because of me, you're gonna get in trouble.
No different than any other day.
At least it's for a good reason this time.
Hey, did you notice there aren't any lights on in here?
The bulbs must have burned out.
We shouldn't stay here long, then. Who knows what's creeping around in here?
I have to find a way to save my grandfather's books.
You're not going to be able to save them all. There are too many.
I'm only interested in the ones he wrote.

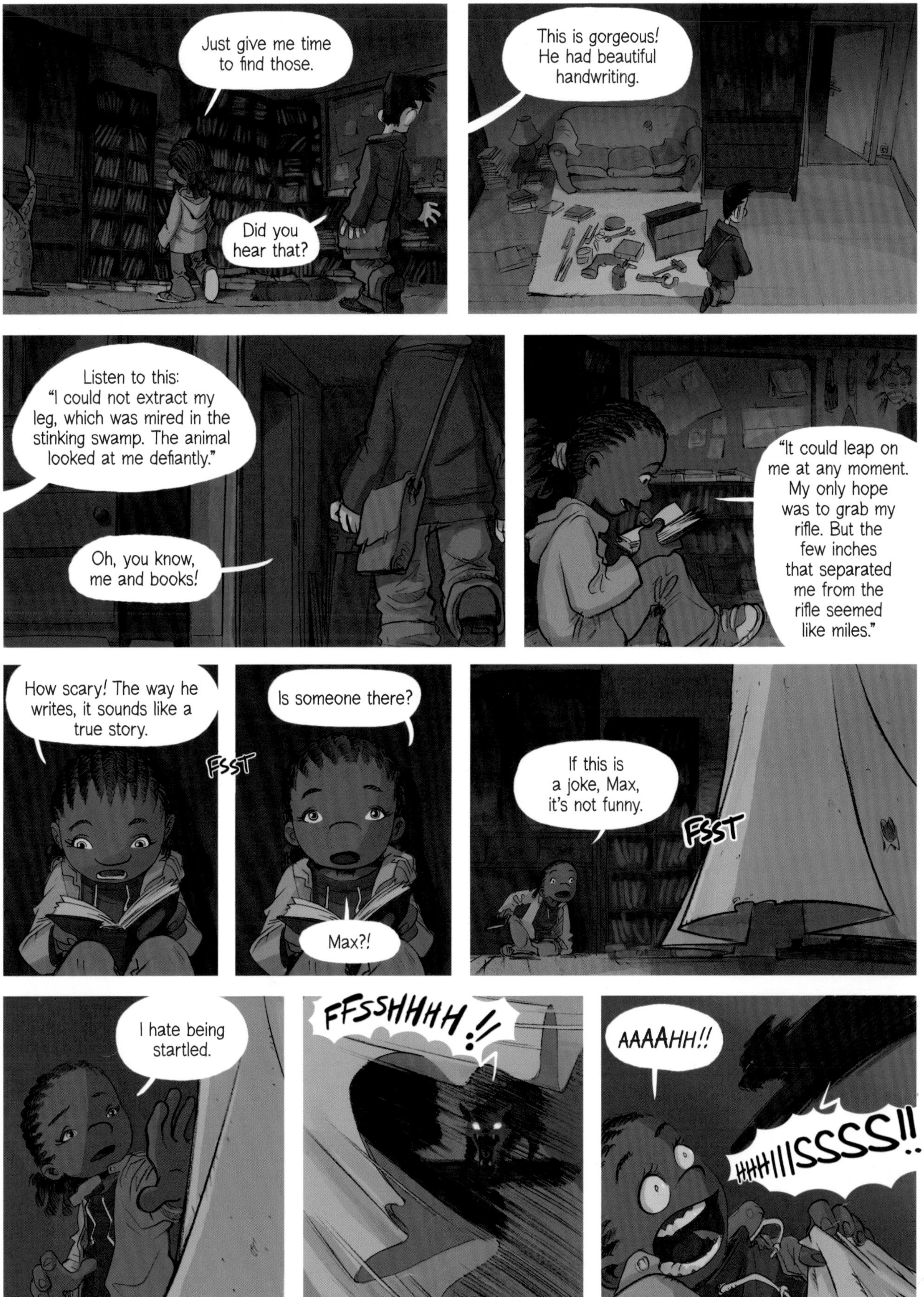

Just give me time to find those.
Did you hear that?
This is gorgeous! He had beautiful handwriting.
Listen to this: "I could not extract my leg, which was mired in the stinking swamp. The animal looked at me defiantly."
Oh, you know, me and books!
"It could leap on me at any moment. My only hope was to grab my rifle. But the few inches that separated me from the rifle seemed like miles."
How scary! The way he writes, it sounds like a true story.
FSST
Is someone there?
Max?!
If this is a joke, Max, it's not funny.
FSST
I hate being startled.
FFSSHHHH!!
AAAAHH!!
HHHIIISSSS!!

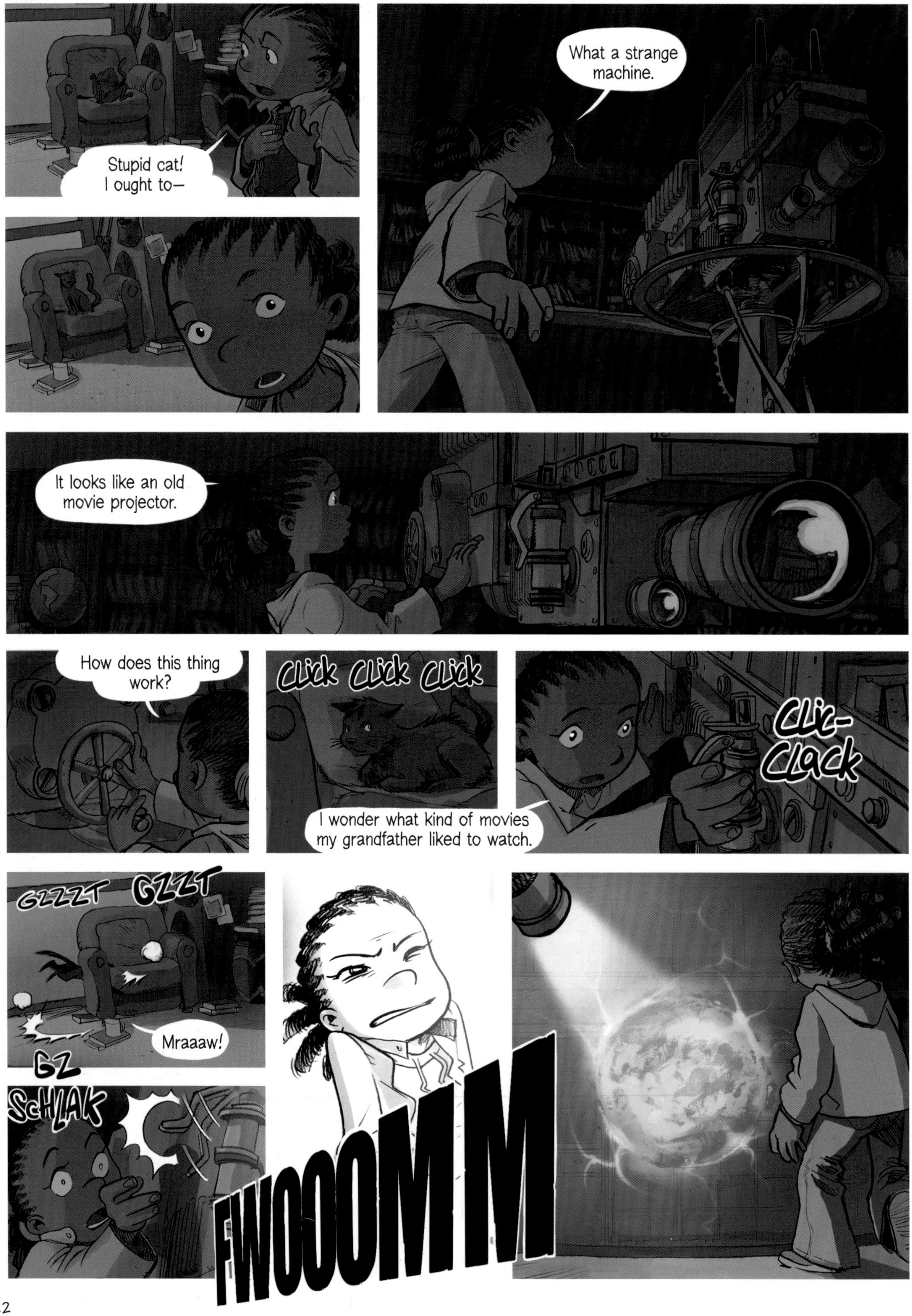
Stupid cat! I ought to—
What a strange machine.
It looks like an old movie projector.
How does this thing work?
Click Click Click
Clic-Clack
I wonder what kind of movies my grandfather liked to watch.
GZZZT GZZT
Mraaaw!
GZ
SCHLAK
FWOOOMM

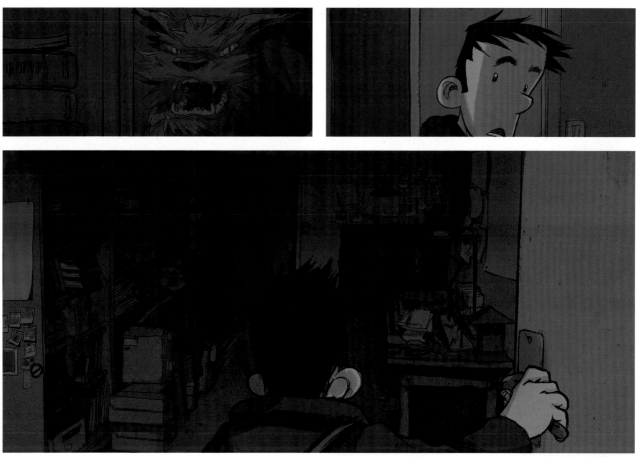

I've never seen a creature like this before…

Noah'd love this for his collection of horrors.

Wow… even more books!

Weirder and weirder…

It looks like a flashlight crossed with a…

DANGER! LIGHT!!

What—?!

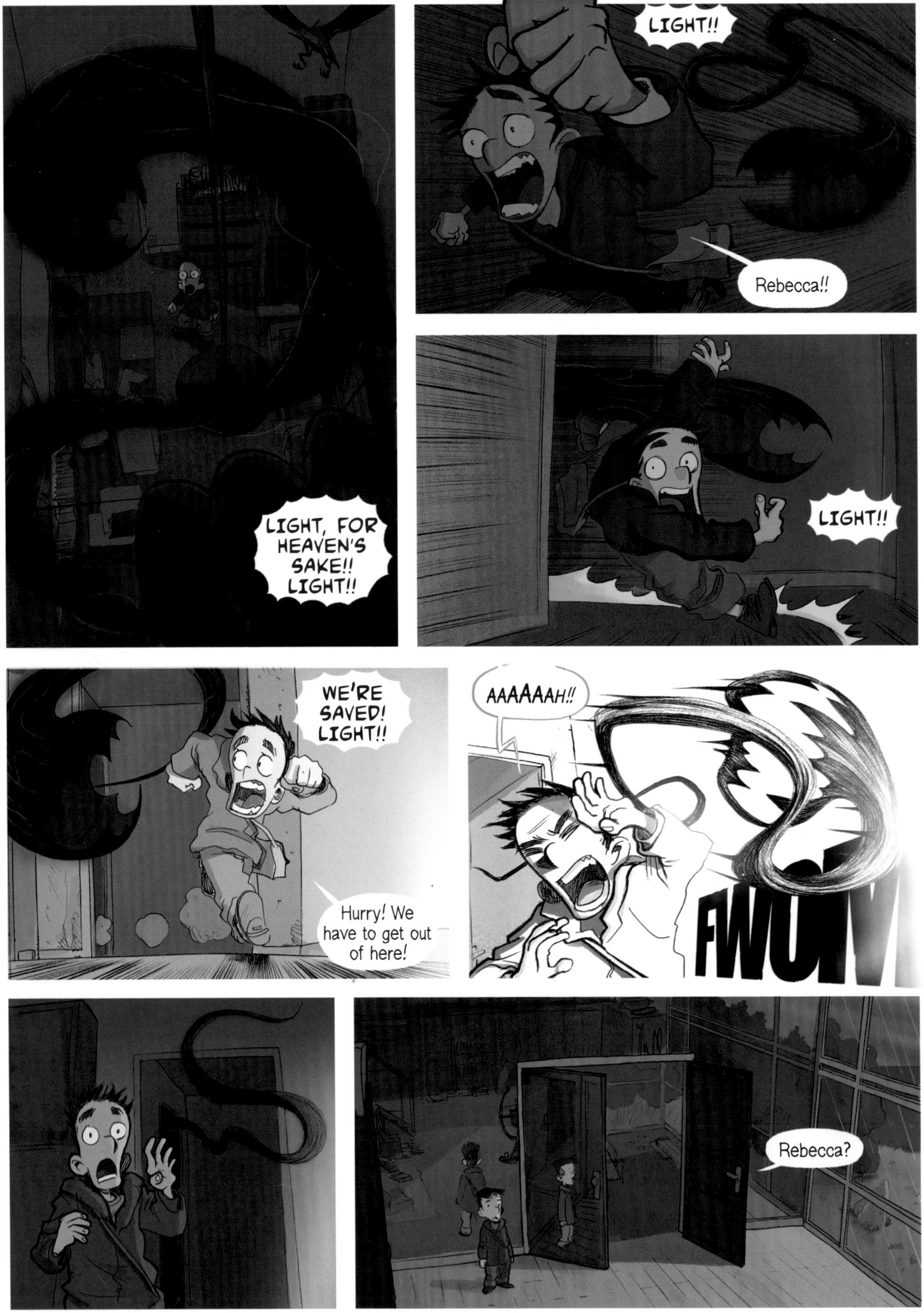
LIGHT, FOR HEAVEN'S SAKE!! LIGHT!!
LIGHT!!
Rebecca!!
LIGHT!!
WE'RE SAVED! LIGHT!!
Hurry! We have to get out of here!
AAAAAAH!!
FWOM
Rebecca?

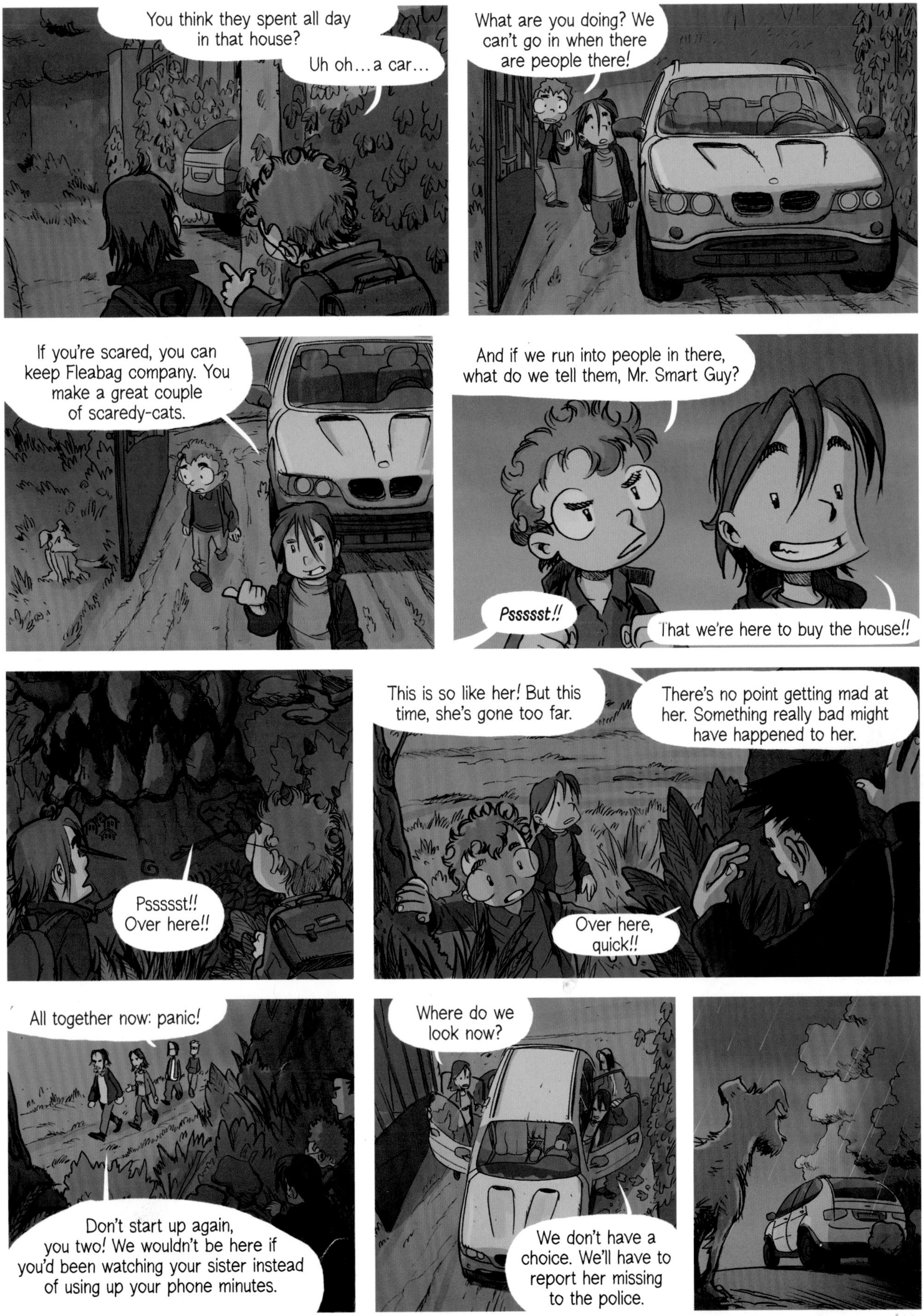
You think they spent all day in that house?
Uh oh... a car...
What are you doing? We can't go in when there are people there!
If you're scared, you can keep Fleabag company. You make a great couple of scaredy-cats.
And if we run into people in there, what do we tell them, Mr. Smart Guy?
Pssssst!!
That we're here to buy the house!!
Pssssst!! Over here!!
This is so like her! But this time, she's gone too far.
There's no point getting mad at her. Something really bad might have happened to her.
Over here, quick!!
All together now: panic!
Don't start up again, you two! We wouldn't be here if you'd been watching your sister instead of using up your phone minutes.
Where do we look now?
We don't have a choice. We'll have to report her missing to the police.

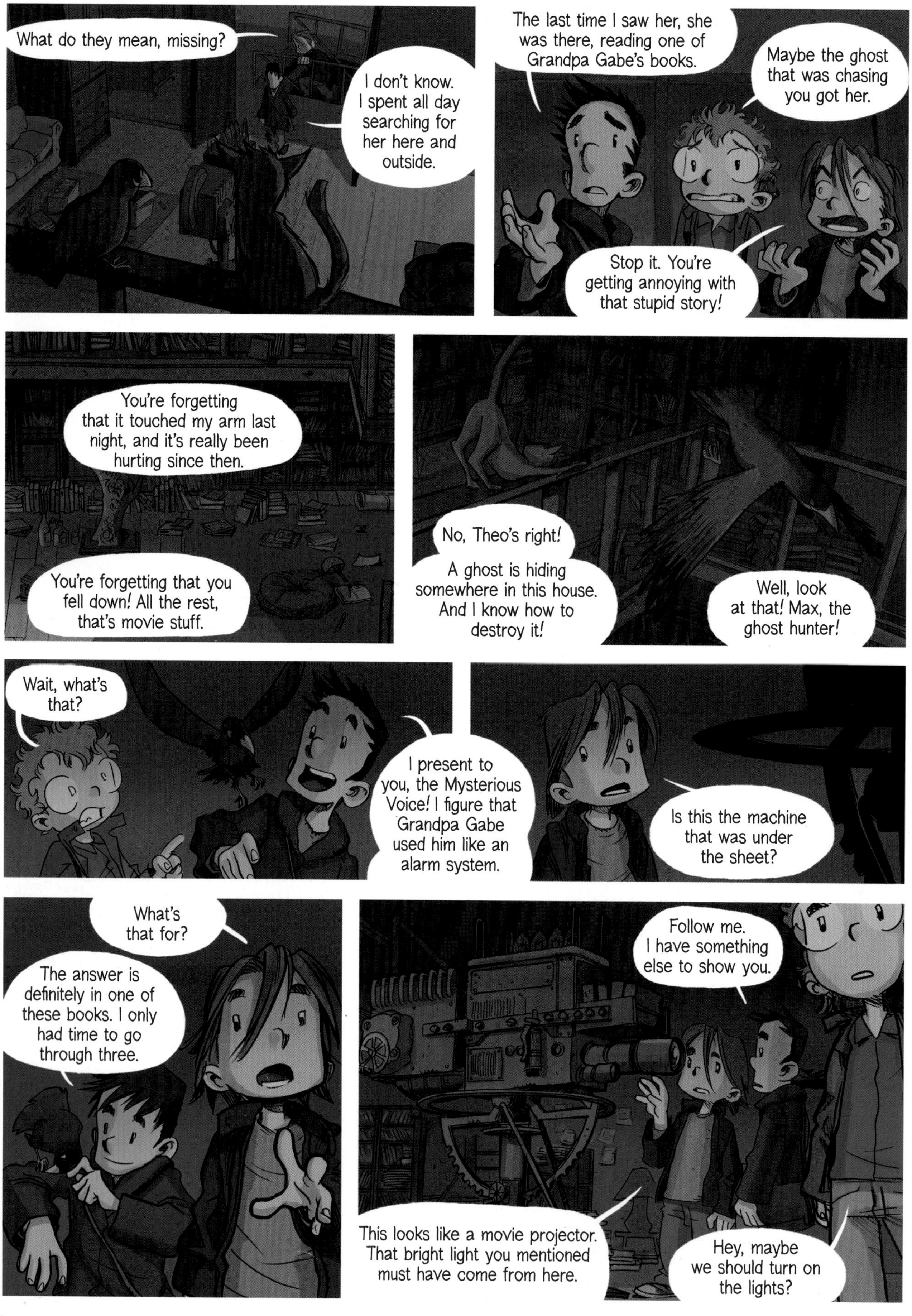

What do they mean, missing?
I don't know. I spent all day searching for her here and outside.
The last time I saw her, she was there, reading one of Grandpa Gabe's books.
Maybe the ghost that was chasing you got her.
Stop it. You're getting annoying with that stupid story!
You're forgetting that it touched my arm last night, and it's really been hurting since then.
You're forgetting that you fell down! All the rest, that's movie stuff.
No, Theo's right!
A ghost is hiding somewhere in this house. And I know how to destroy it!
Well, look at that! Max, the ghost hunter!
Wait, what's that?
I present to you, the Mysterious Voice! I figure that Grandpa Gabe used him like an alarm system.
Is this the machine that was under the sheet?
What's that for?
The answer is definitely in one of these books. I only had time to go through three.
Follow me. I have something else to show you.
This looks like a movie projector. That bright light you mentioned must have come from here.
Hey, maybe we should turn on the lights?

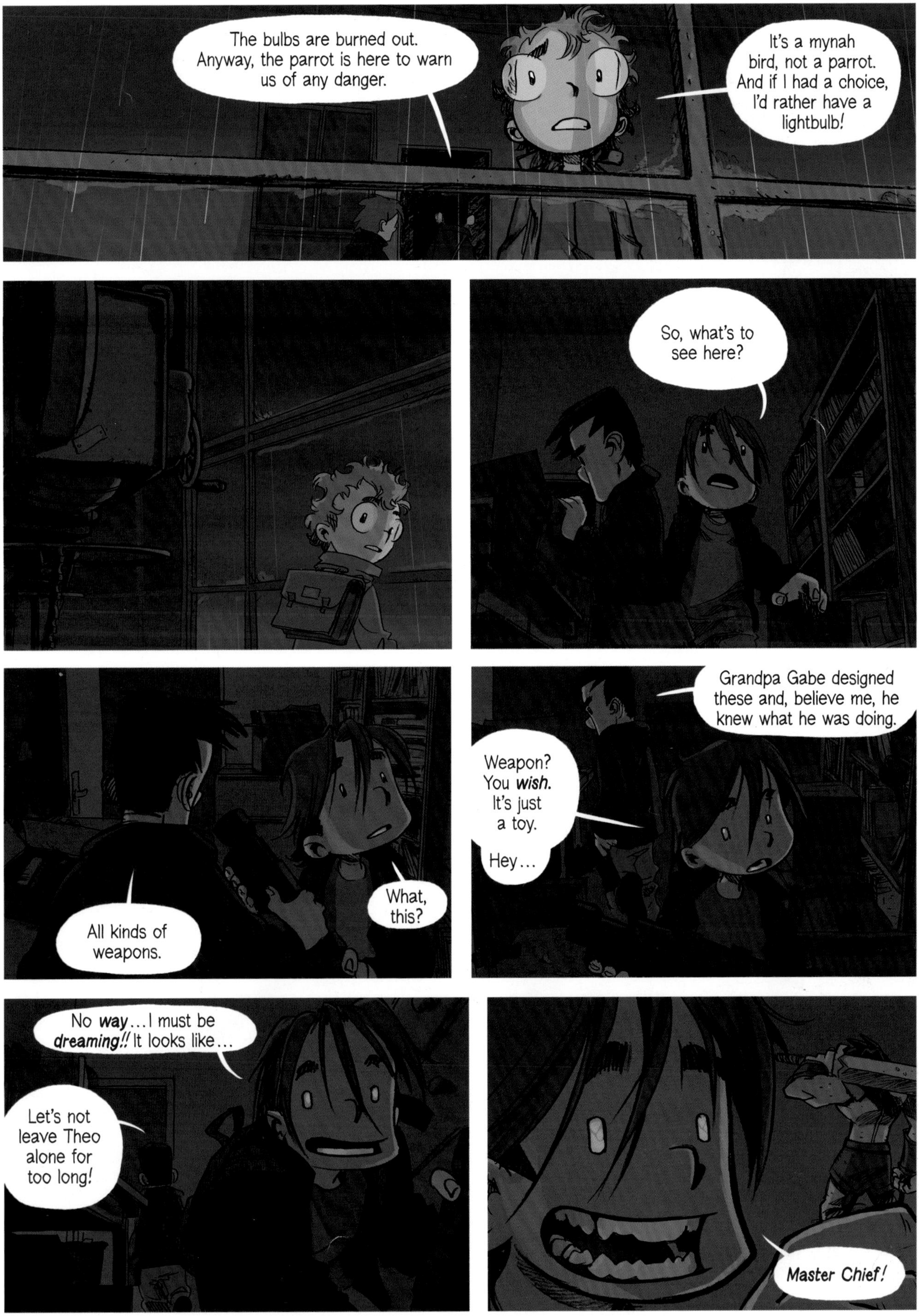
The bulbs are burned out. Anyway, the parrot is here to warn us of any danger.
It's a mynah bird, not a parrot. And if I had a choice, I'd rather have a lightbulb!
So, what's to see here?
All kinds of weapons.
What, this?
Grandpa Gabe designed these and, believe me, he knew what he was doing.
Weapon? You *wish.* It's just a toy.
Hey...
No **way**... I must be ***dreaming!!*** It looks like...
Let's not leave Theo alone for too long!
Master Chief!

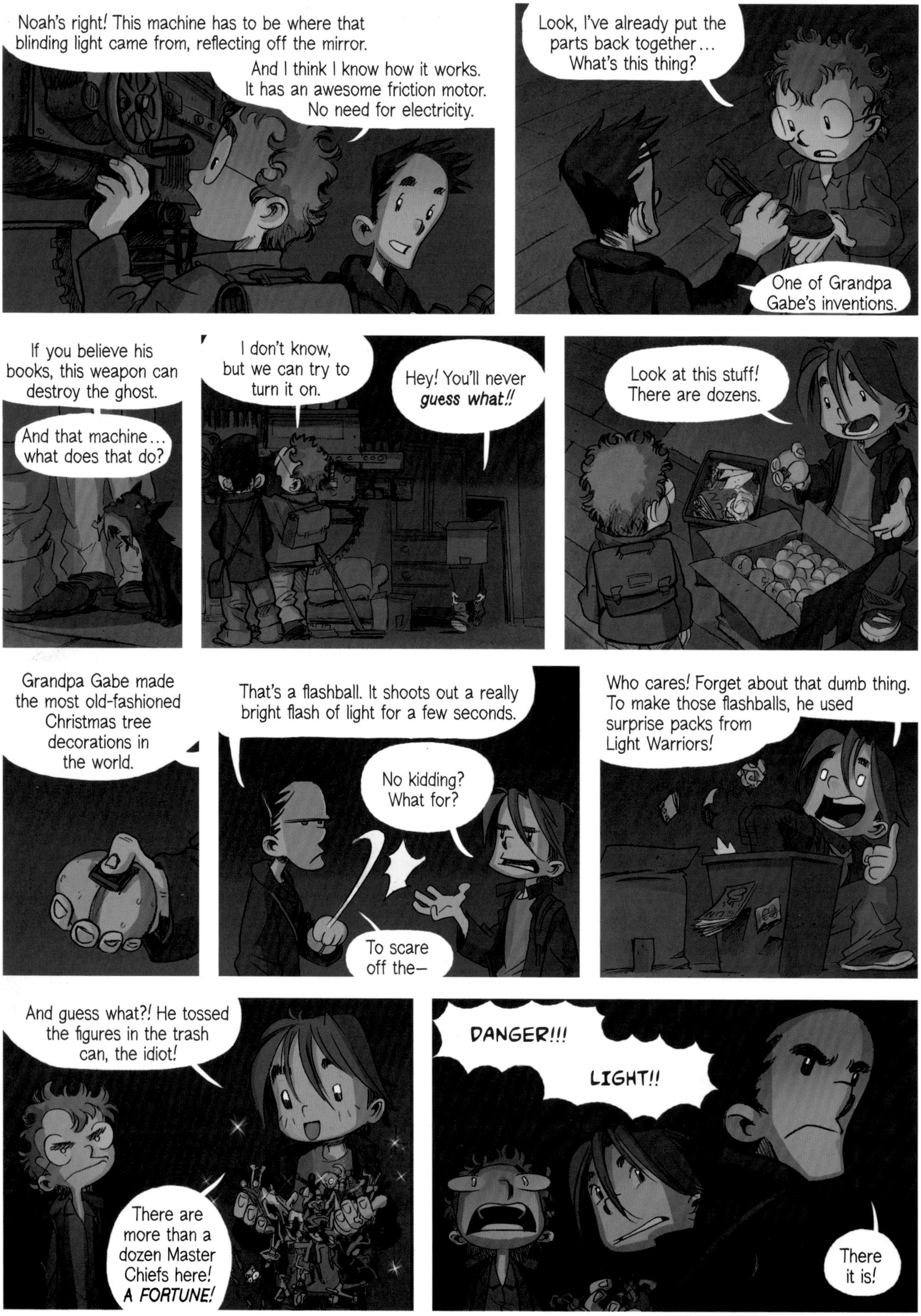

Noah's right! This machine has to be where that blinding light came from, reflecting off the mirror.
And I think I know how it works. It has an awesome friction motor. No need for electricity.
Look, I've already put the parts back together... What's this thing?
One of Grandpa Gabe's inventions.
If you believe his books, this weapon can destroy the ghost.
And that machine... what does that do?
I don't know, but we can try to turn it on.
Hey! You'll never *guess what!!*
Look at this stuff! There are dozens.
Grandpa Gabe made the most old-fashioned Christmas tree decorations in the world.
That's a flashball. It shoots out a really bright flash of light for a few seconds.
No kidding? What for?
To scare off the—
Who cares! Forget about that dumb thing. To make those flashballs, he used surprise packs from Light Warriors!
And guess what?! He tossed the figures in the trash can, the idiot!
There are more than a dozen Master Chiefs here! *A FORTUNE!*
DANGER!!!
LIGHT!!
There it is!

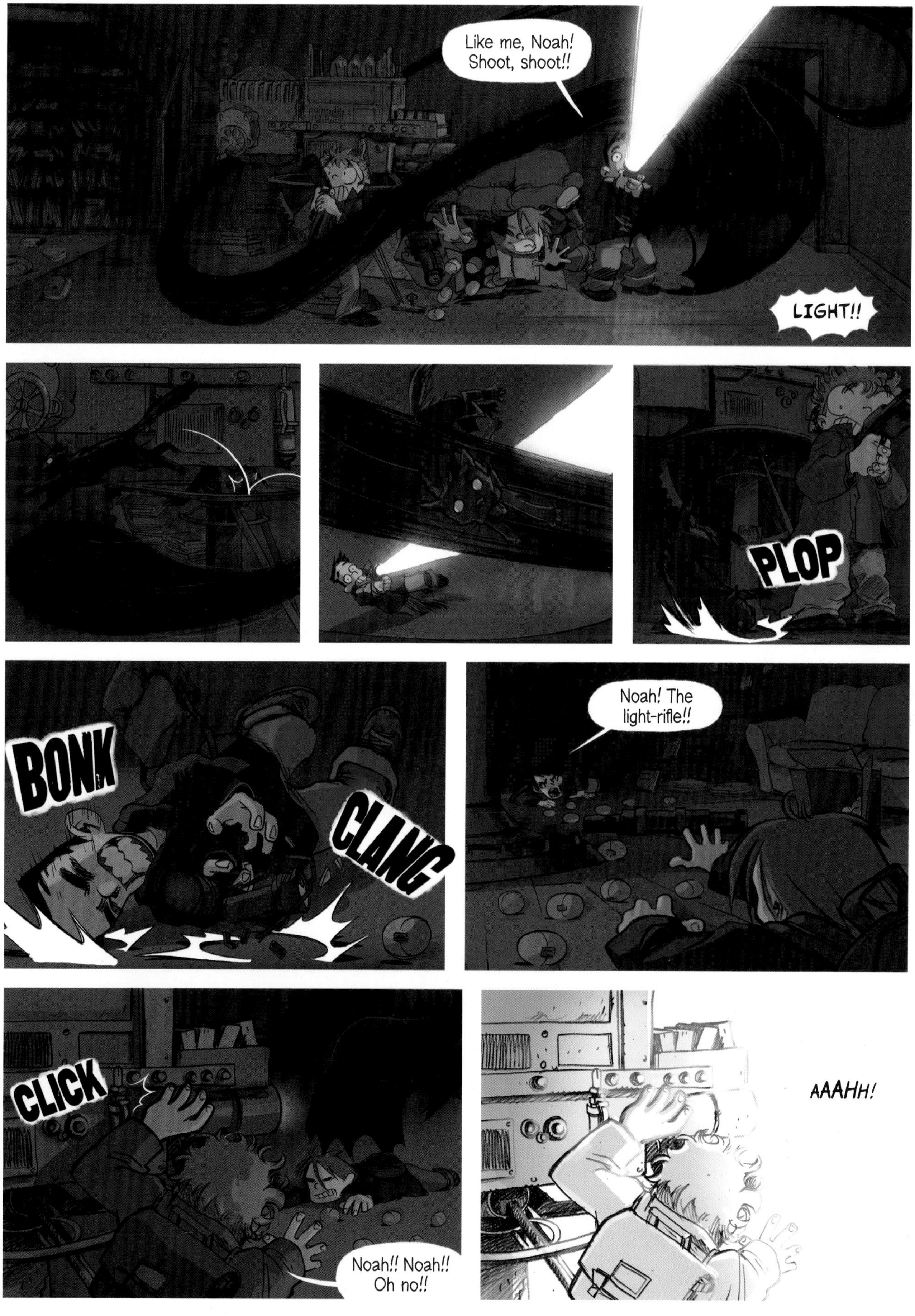
Like me, Noah!
Shoot, shoot!!
LIGHT!!
PLOP
BONK
CLANG
Noah! The light-rifle!!
CLICK
Noah!! Noah!! Oh no!!
AAAHH!

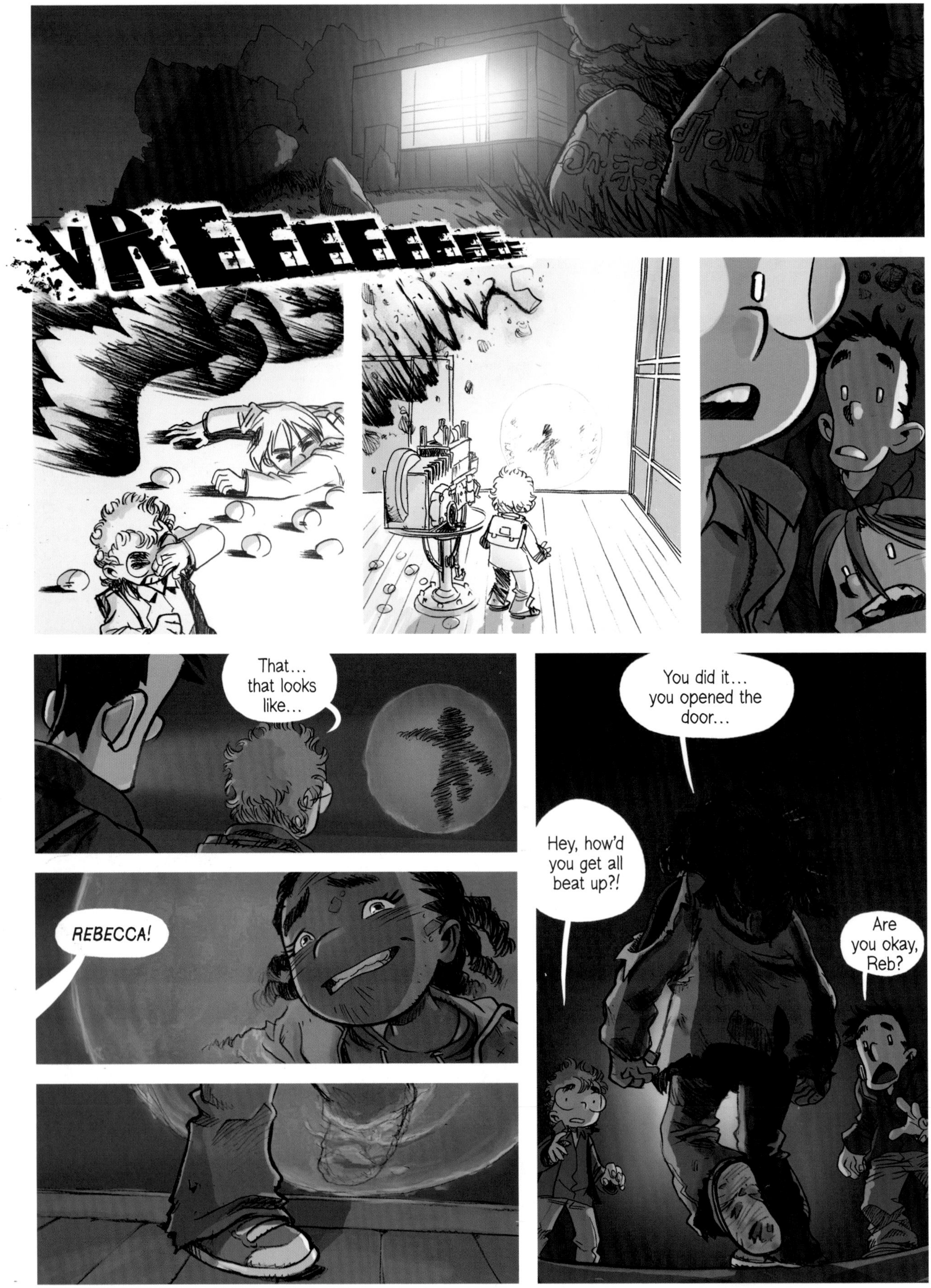
VREEEEEEE...
That... that looks like...
REBECCA!
You did it... you opened the door...
Hey, how'd you get all beat up?!
Are you okay, Reb?

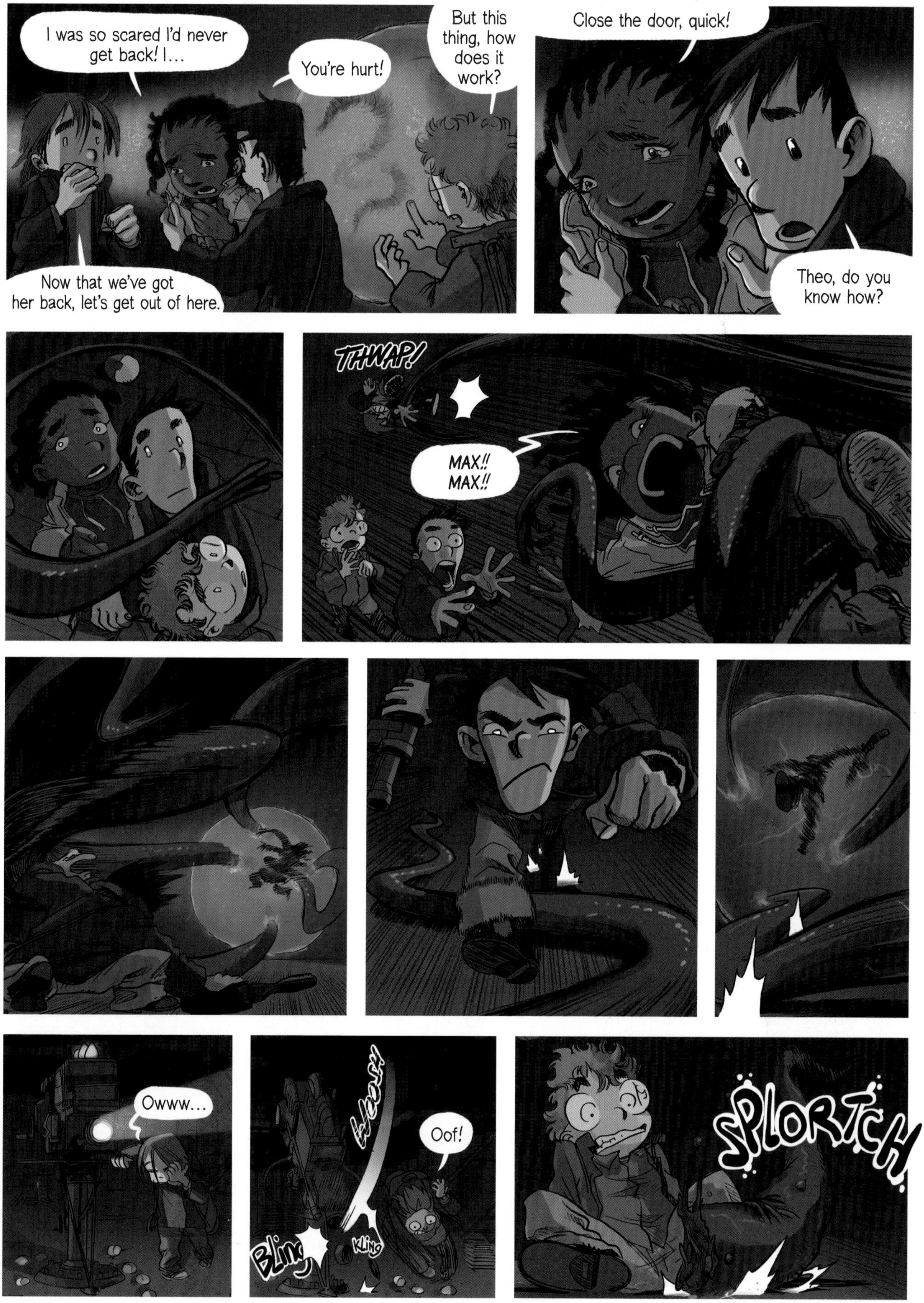
I was so scared I'd never get back! I...
You're hurt!
But this thing, how does it work?
Now that we've got her back, let's get out of here.
Close the door, quick!
Theo, do you know how?
THWAP!
MAX!! MAX!!
Owww...
WOOSH
Oof!
Bling
KLING
SPLORTCH

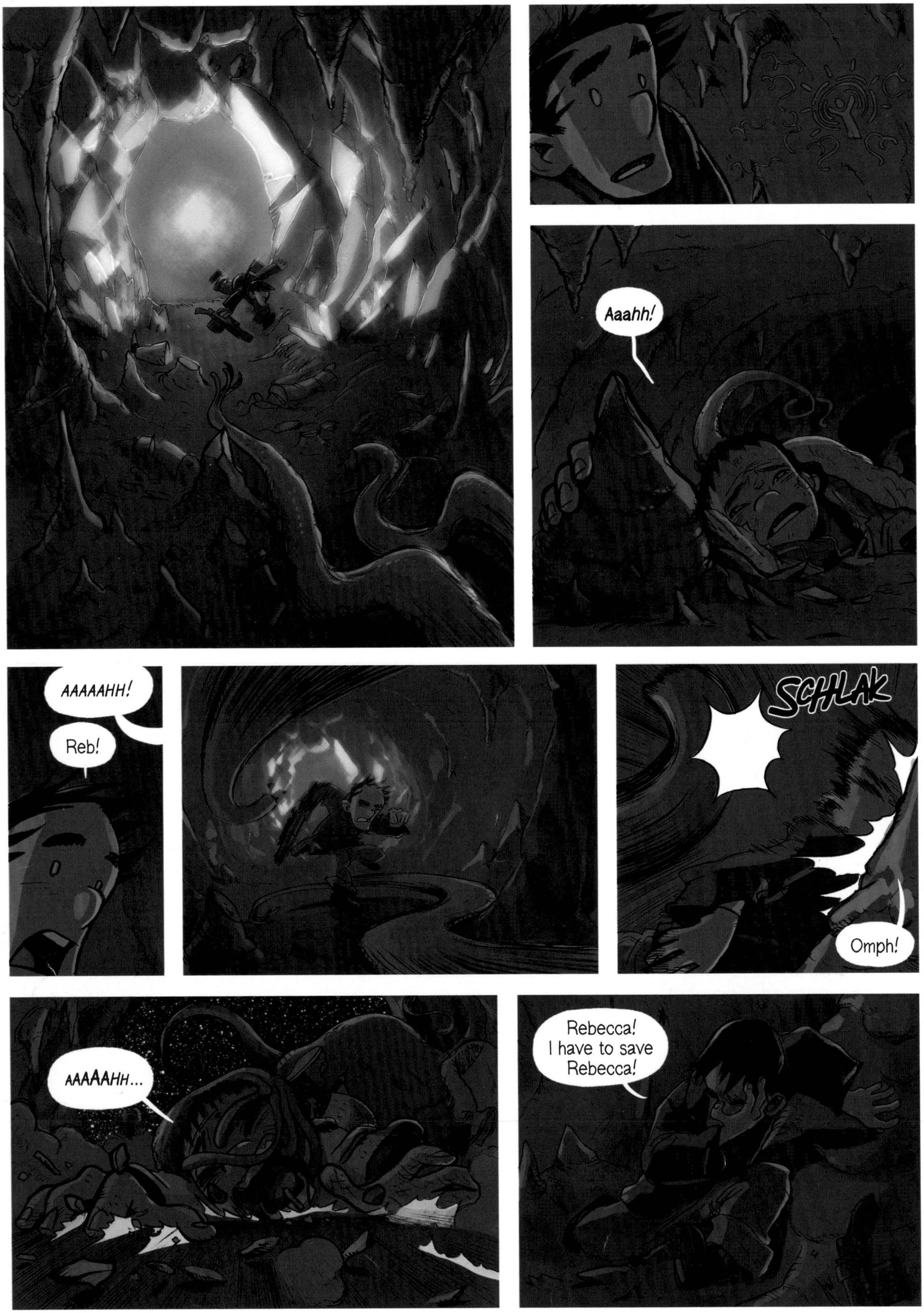
Aaahh!
AAAAAHH!
Reb!
SCHLAK
Omph!
AAAAAHH...
Rebecca!
I have to save
Rebecca!

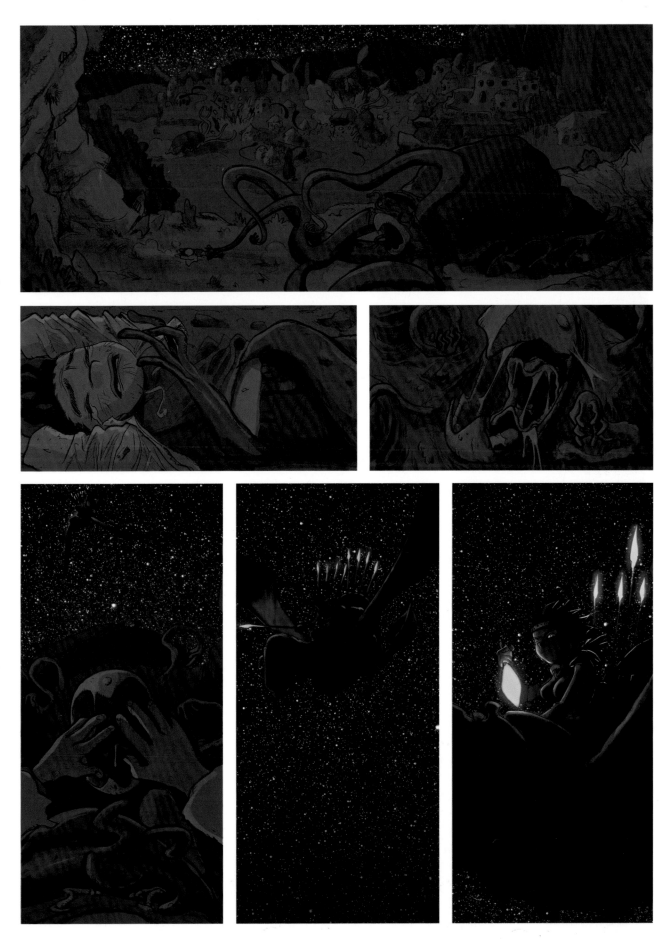

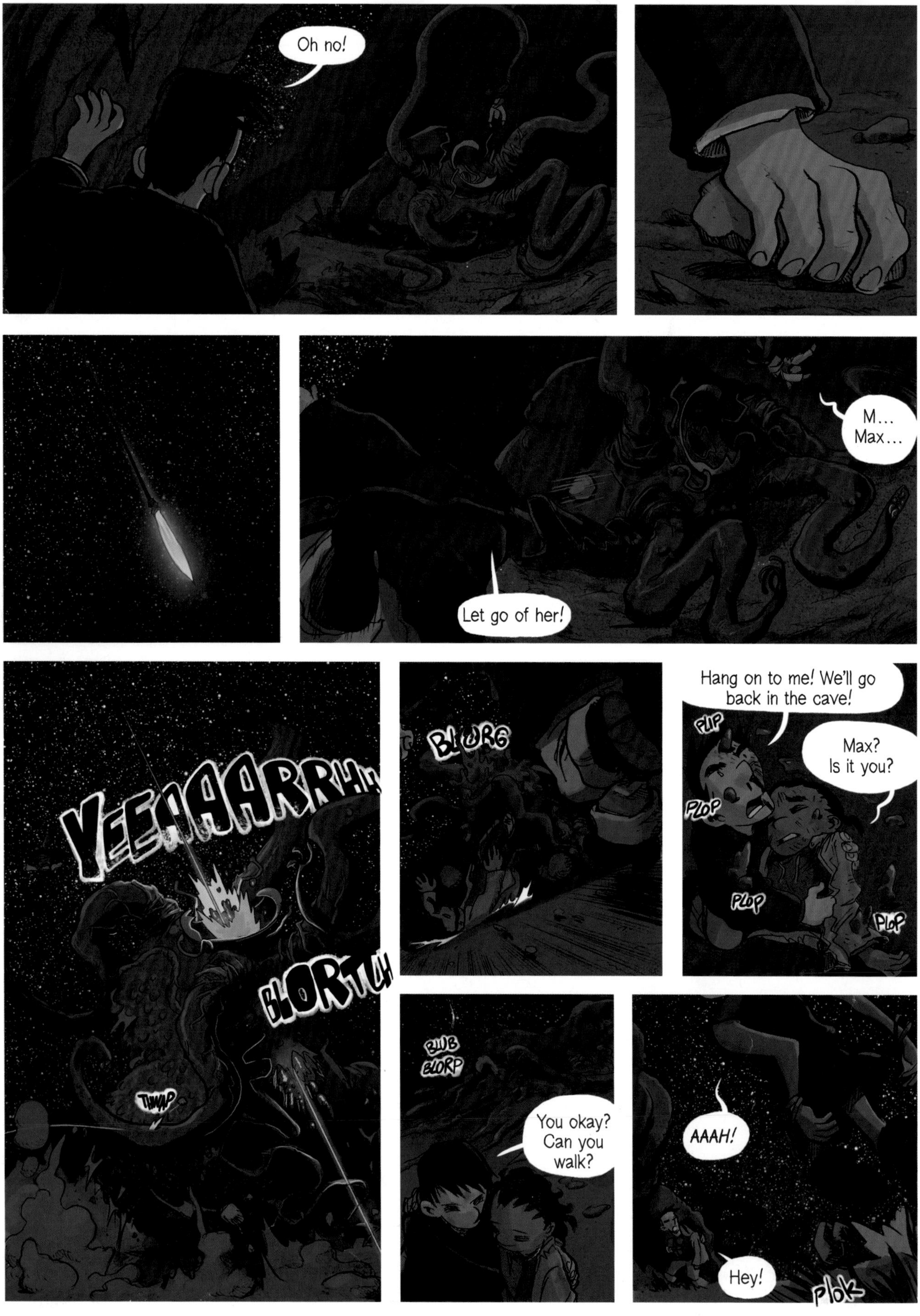
Oh no!
M...
Max...
Let go of her!
YEEAAARRH!
BLORTCH
THWAP
BLURG
Hang on to me! We'll go back in the cave!
PLIP
Max?
Is it you?
PLOP
PLOP
PLOP
BLUB
BLORP
You okay? Can you walk?
AAAH!
Hey!
PLOK

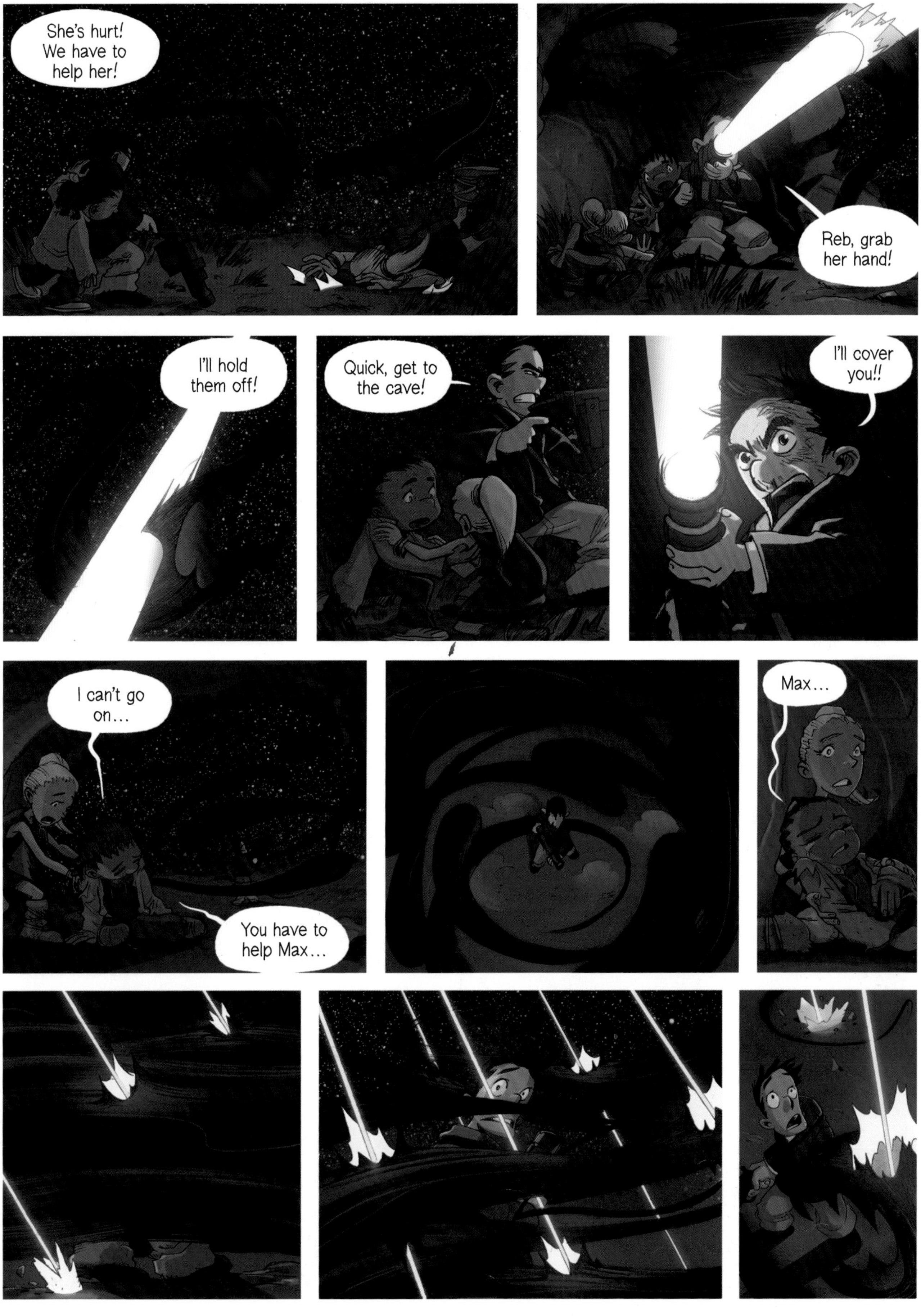

She's hurt! We have to help her!
Reb, grab her hand!
I'll hold them off!
Quick, get to the cave!
I'll cover you!!
I can't go on...
You have to help Max...
Max...

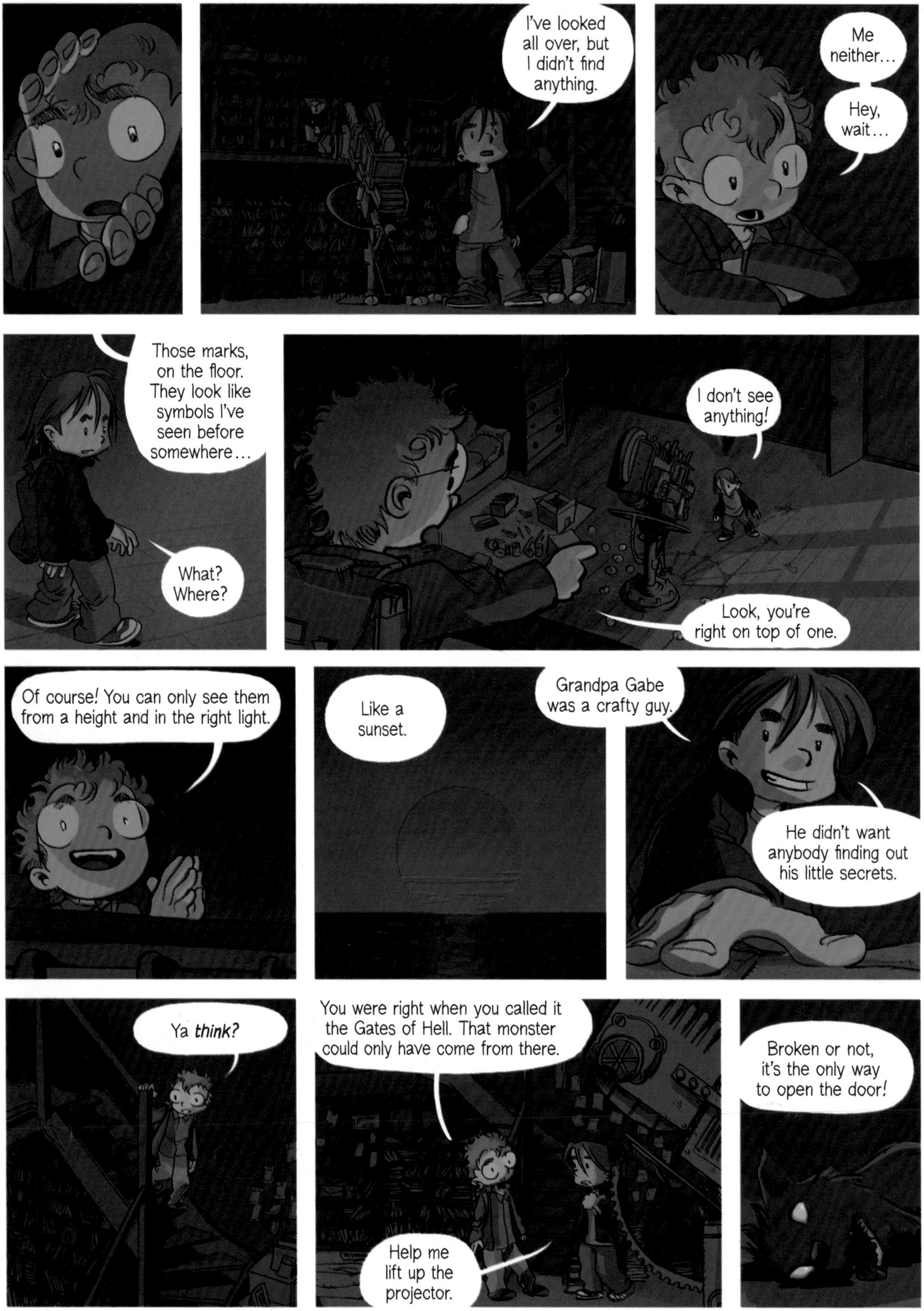
I've looked all over, but I didn't find anything.
Me neither...
Hey, wait...
Those marks, on the floor. They look like symbols I've seen before somewhere...
What? Where?
I don't see anything!
Look, you're right on top of one.
Of course! You can only see them from a height and in the right light.
Like a sunset.
Grandpa Gabe was a crafty guy.
He didn't want anybody finding out his little secrets.
Ya *think?*
You were right when you called it the Gates of Hell. That monster could only have come from there.
Help me lift up the projector.
Broken or not, it's the only way to open the door!

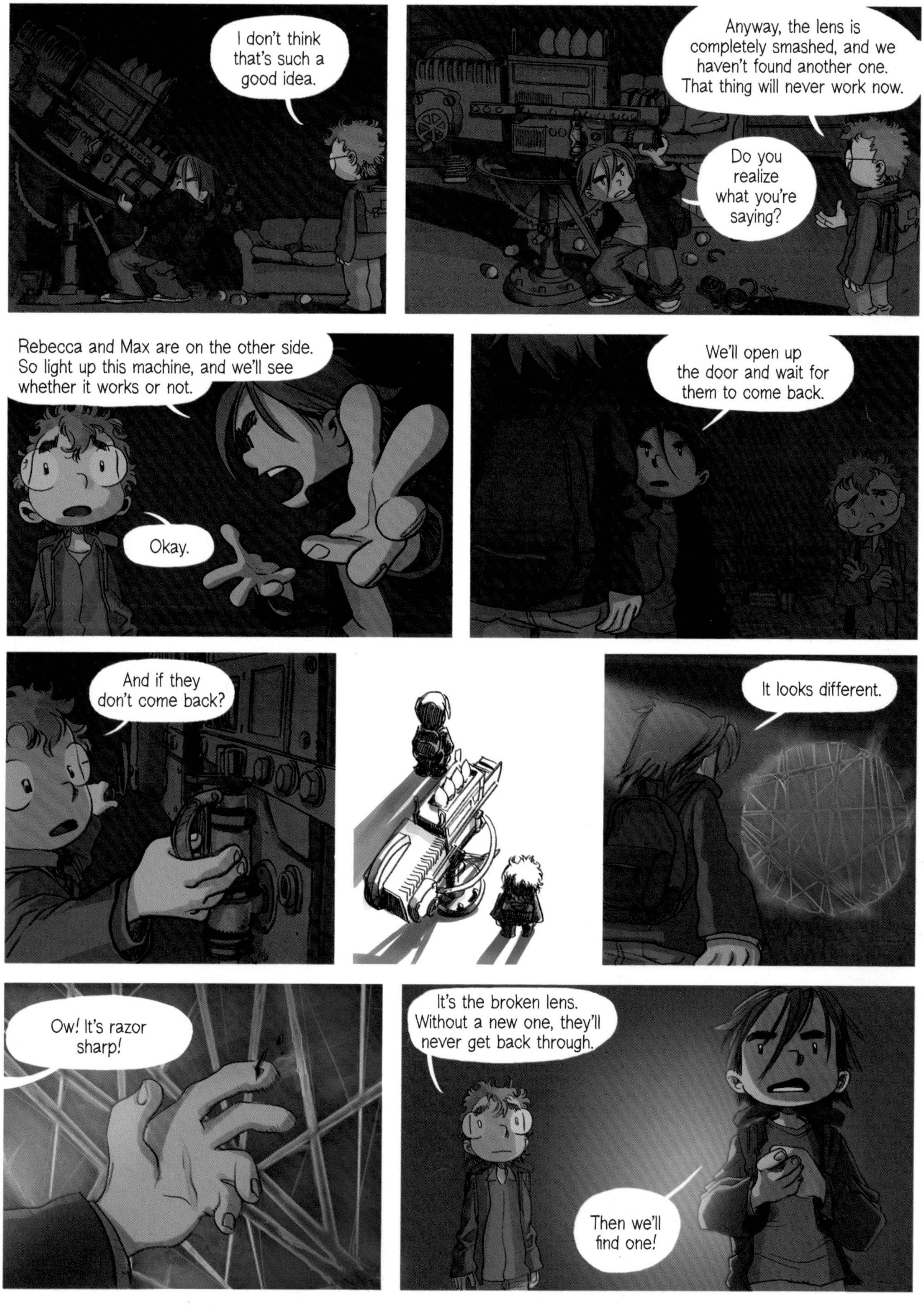
I don't think that's such a good idea.
Anyway, the lens is completely smashed, and we haven't found another one. That thing will never work now.
Do you realize what you're saying?
Rebecca and Max are on the other side. So light up this machine, and we'll see whether it works or not.
Okay.
We'll open up the door and wait for them to come back.
And if they don't come back?
It looks different.
Ow! It's razor sharp!
It's the broken lens. Without a new one, they'll never get back through.
Then we'll find one!

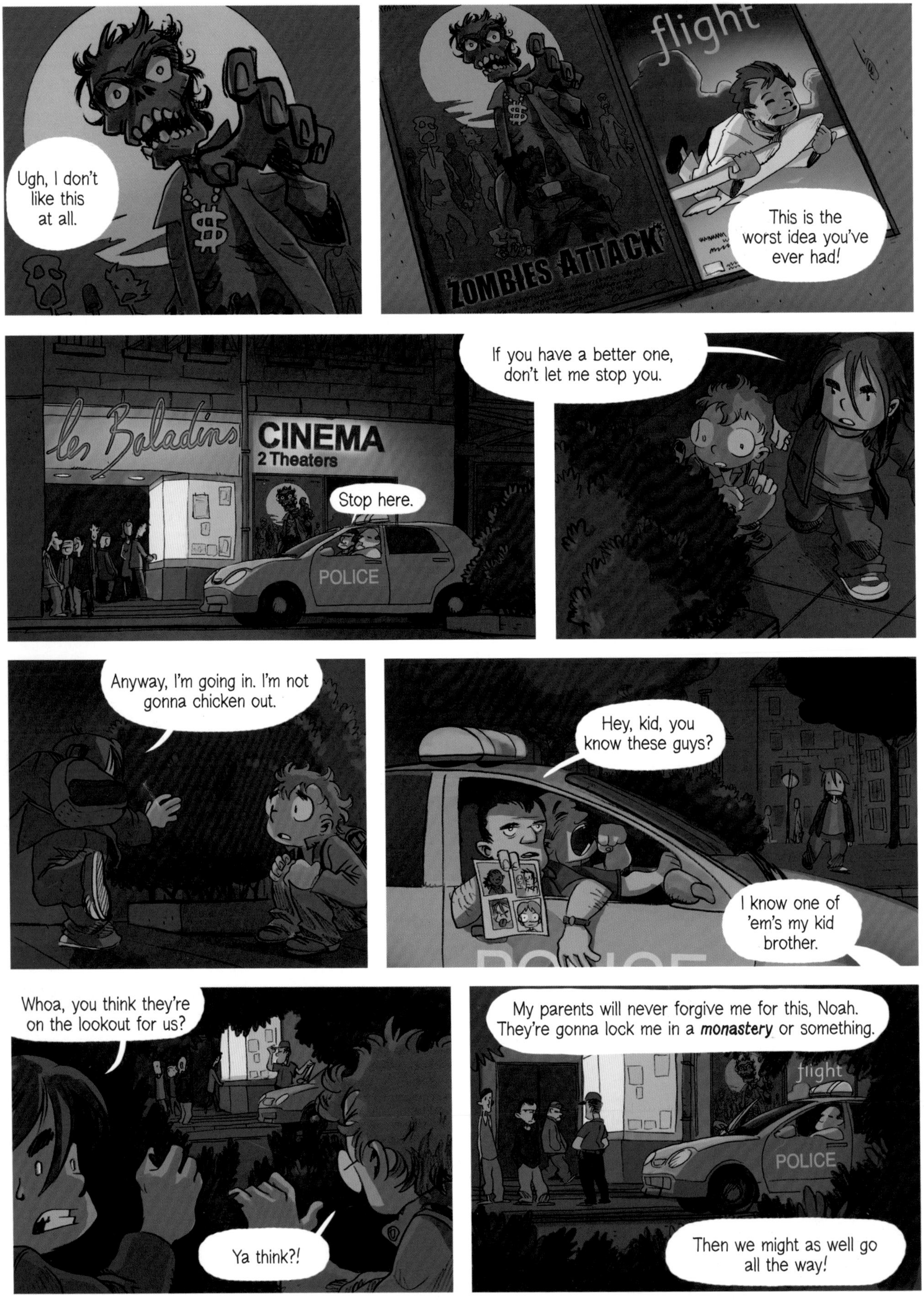

Ugh, I don't like this at all.
flight
ZOMBIES ATTACK
This is the worst idea you've ever had!
les Baladins
CINEMA
2 Theaters
Stop here.
POLICE
If you have a better one, don't let me stop you.
Anyway, I'm going in. I'm not gonna chicken out.
Hey, kid, you know these guys?
I know one of 'em's my kid brother.
Whoa, you think they're on the lookout for us?
Ya think?!
My parents will never forgive me for this, Noah. They're gonna lock me in a ***monastery*** or something.
flight
POLICE
Then we might as well go all the way!

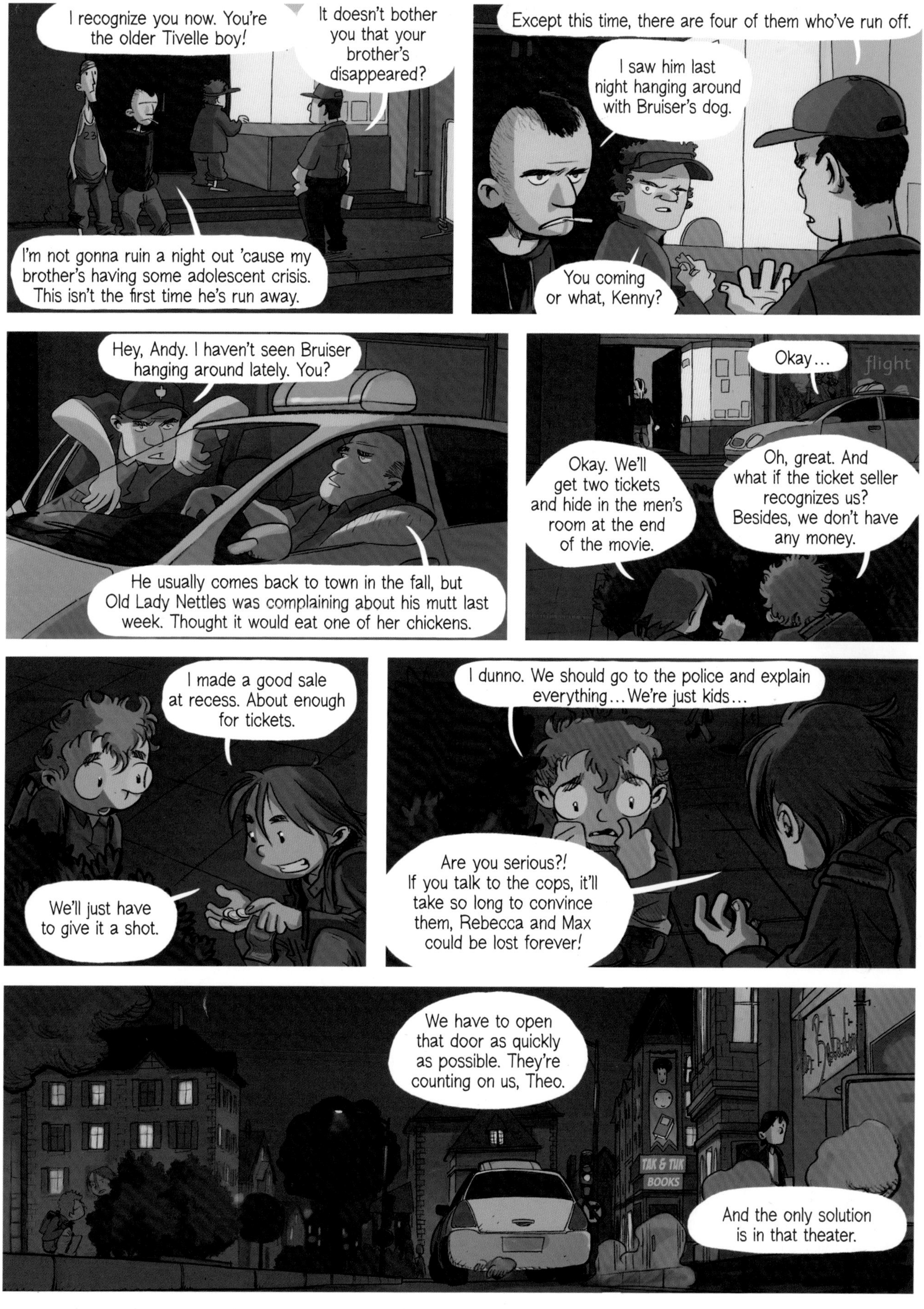
I recognize you now. You're the older Tivelle boy!
It doesn't bother you that your brother's disappeared?
I'm not gonna ruin a night out 'cause my brother's having some adolescent crisis. This isn't the first time he's run away.
Except this time, there are four of them who've run off.
I saw him last night hanging around with Bruiser's dog.
You coming or what, Kenny?
Hey, Andy. I haven't seen Bruiser hanging around lately. You?
He usually comes back to town in the fall, but Old Lady Nettles was complaining about his mutt last week. Thought it would eat one of her chickens.
Okay…
Okay. We'll get two tickets and hide in the men's room at the end of the movie.
Oh, great. And what if the ticket seller recognizes us? Besides, we don't have any money.
I made a good sale at recess. About enough for tickets.
We'll just have to give it a shot.
I dunno. We should go to the police and explain everything… We're just kids…
Are you serious?! If you talk to the cops, it'll take so long to convince them, Rebecca and Max could be lost forever!
We have to open that door as quickly as possible. They're counting on us, Theo.
TAK & TAK BOOKS
And the only solution is in that theater.

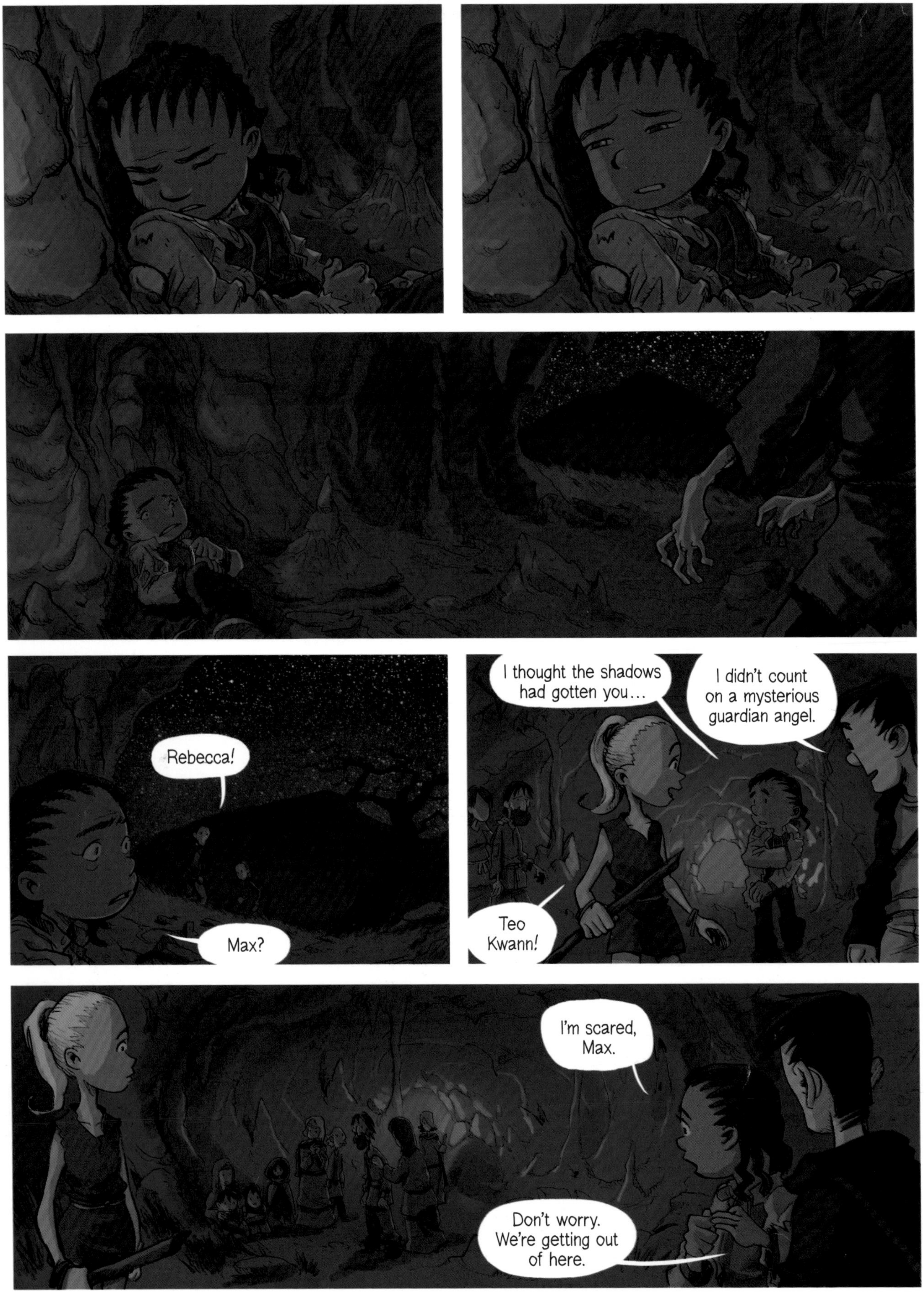
Rebecca!
Max?
I thought the shadows had gotten you…
I didn't count on a mysterious guardian angel.
Teo Kwann!
I'm scared, Max.
Don't worry. We're getting out of here.

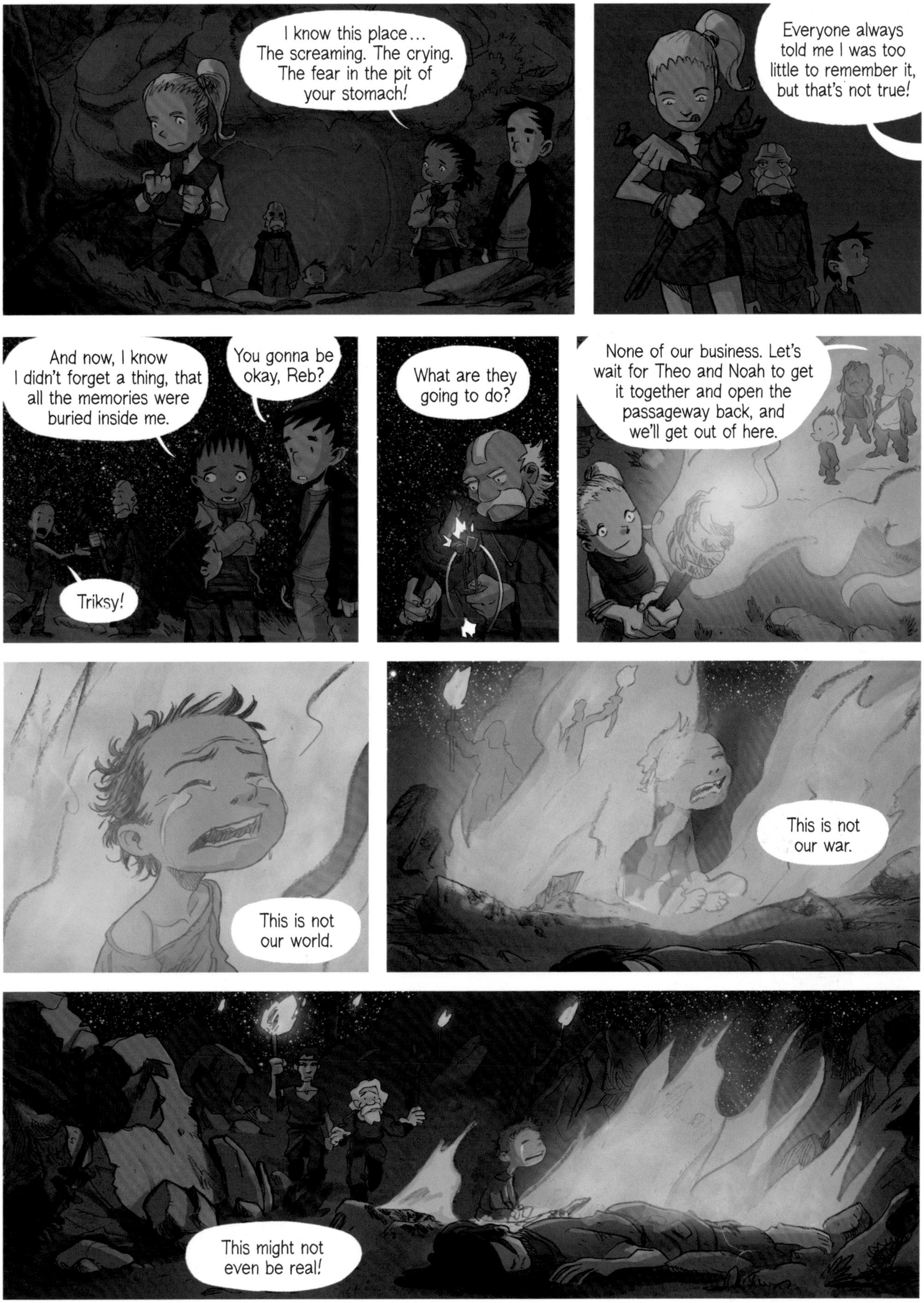
I know this place... The screaming. The crying. The fear in the pit of your stomach!
Everyone always told me I was too little to remember it, but that's not true!
And now, I know I didn't forget a thing, that all the memories were buried inside me.
You gonna be okay, Reb?
Triksy!
What are they going to do?
None of our business. Let's wait for Theo and Noah to get it together and open the passageway back, and we'll get out of here.
This is not our world.
This is not our war.
This might not even be real!

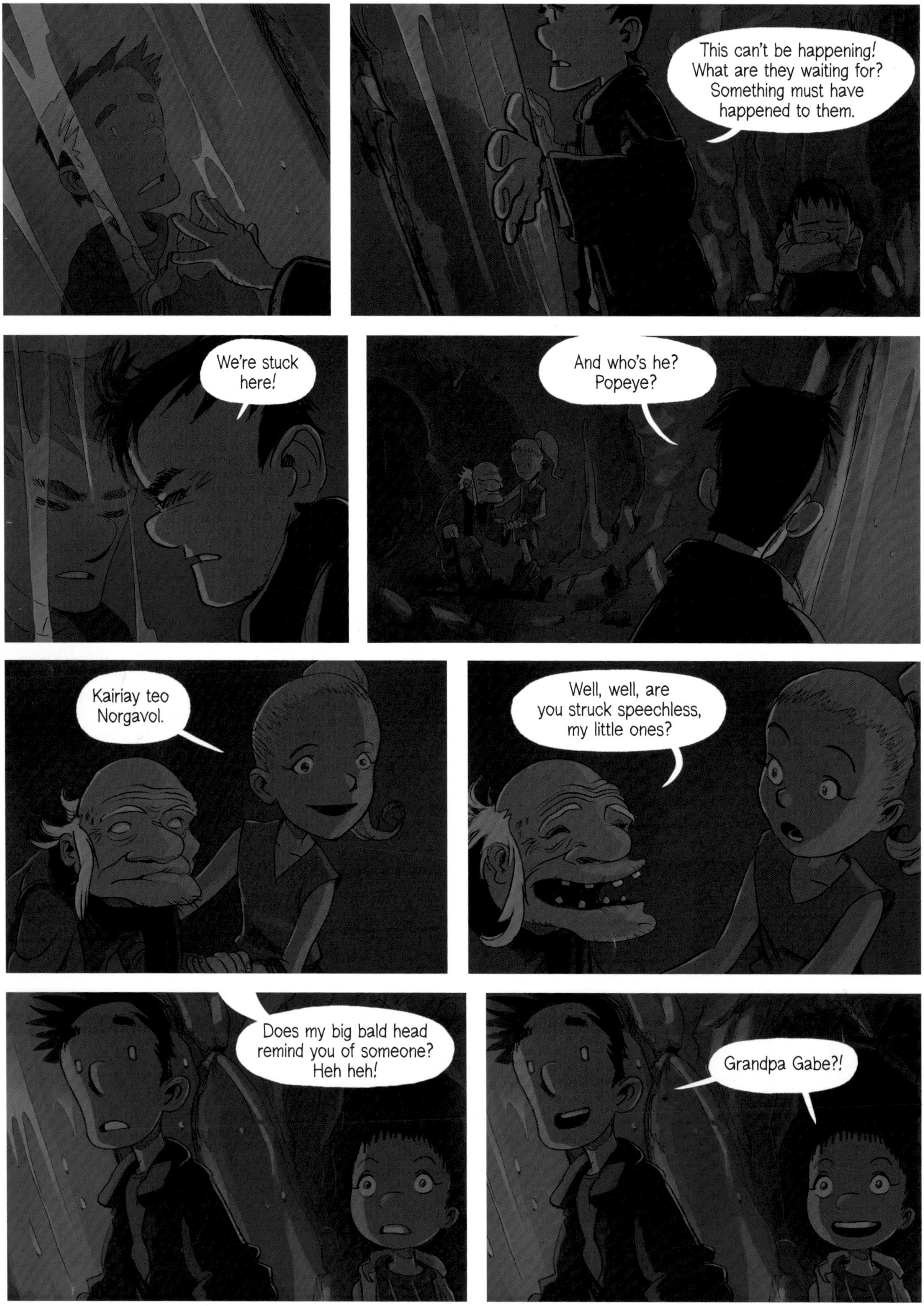
This can't be happening! What are they waiting for? Something must have happened to them.
We're stuck here!
And who's he? Popeye?
Kairiay teo Norgavol.
Well, well, are you struck speechless, my little ones?
Does my big bald head remind you of someone? Heh heh!
Grandpa Gabe?!

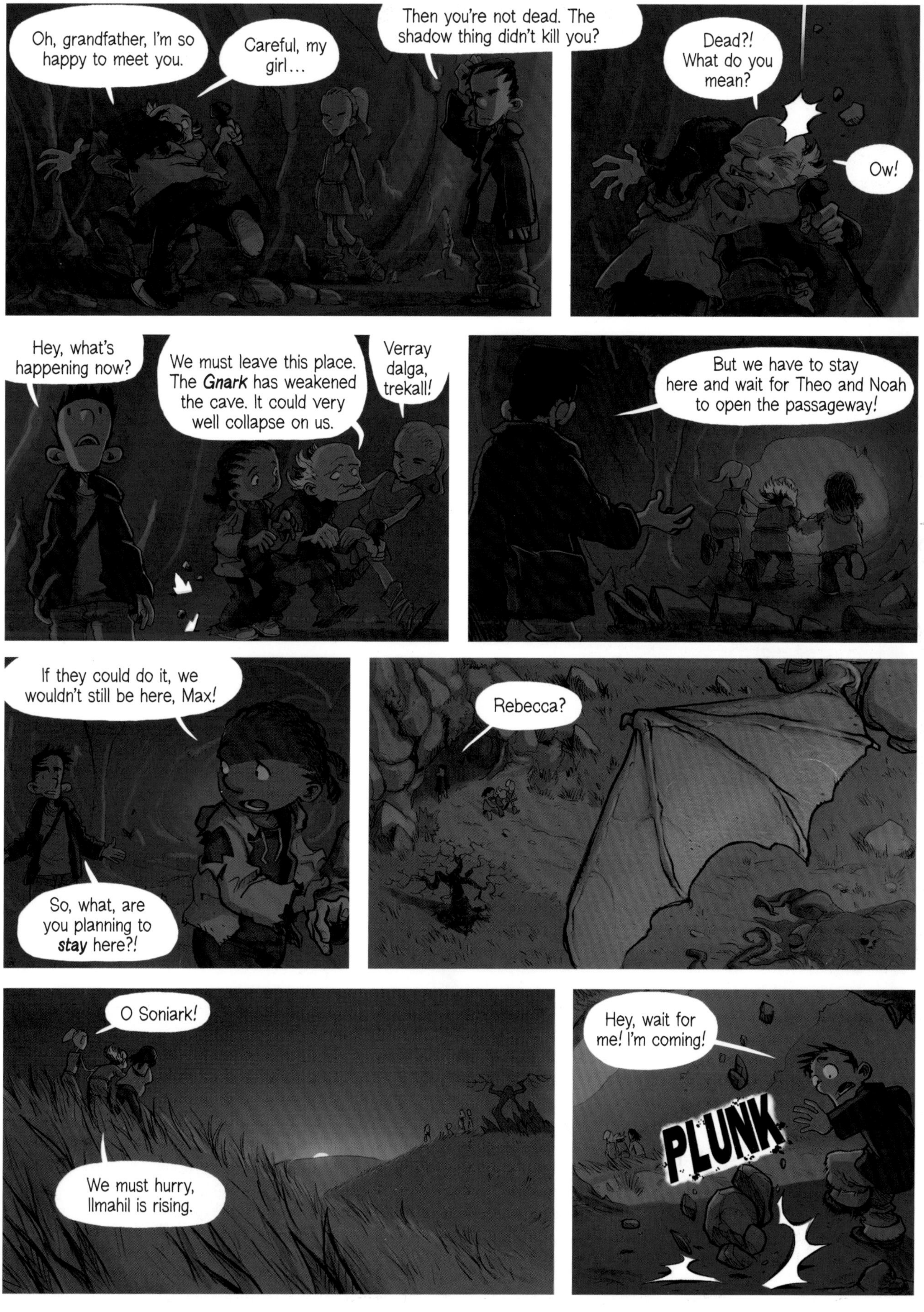
Oh, grandfather, I'm so happy to meet you.
Careful, my girl...
Then you're not dead. The shadow thing didn't kill you?
Dead?! What do you mean?
Ow!
Hey, what's happening now?
We must leave this place. The Gnark has weakened the cave. It could very well collapse on us.
Verray dalga, trekall!
But we have to stay here and wait for Theo and Noah to open the passageway!
If they could do it, we wouldn't still be here, Max!
So, what, are you planning to stay here?!
Rebecca?
O Soniark!
We must hurry, Ilmahil is rising.
Hey, wait for me! I'm coming!
PLUNK

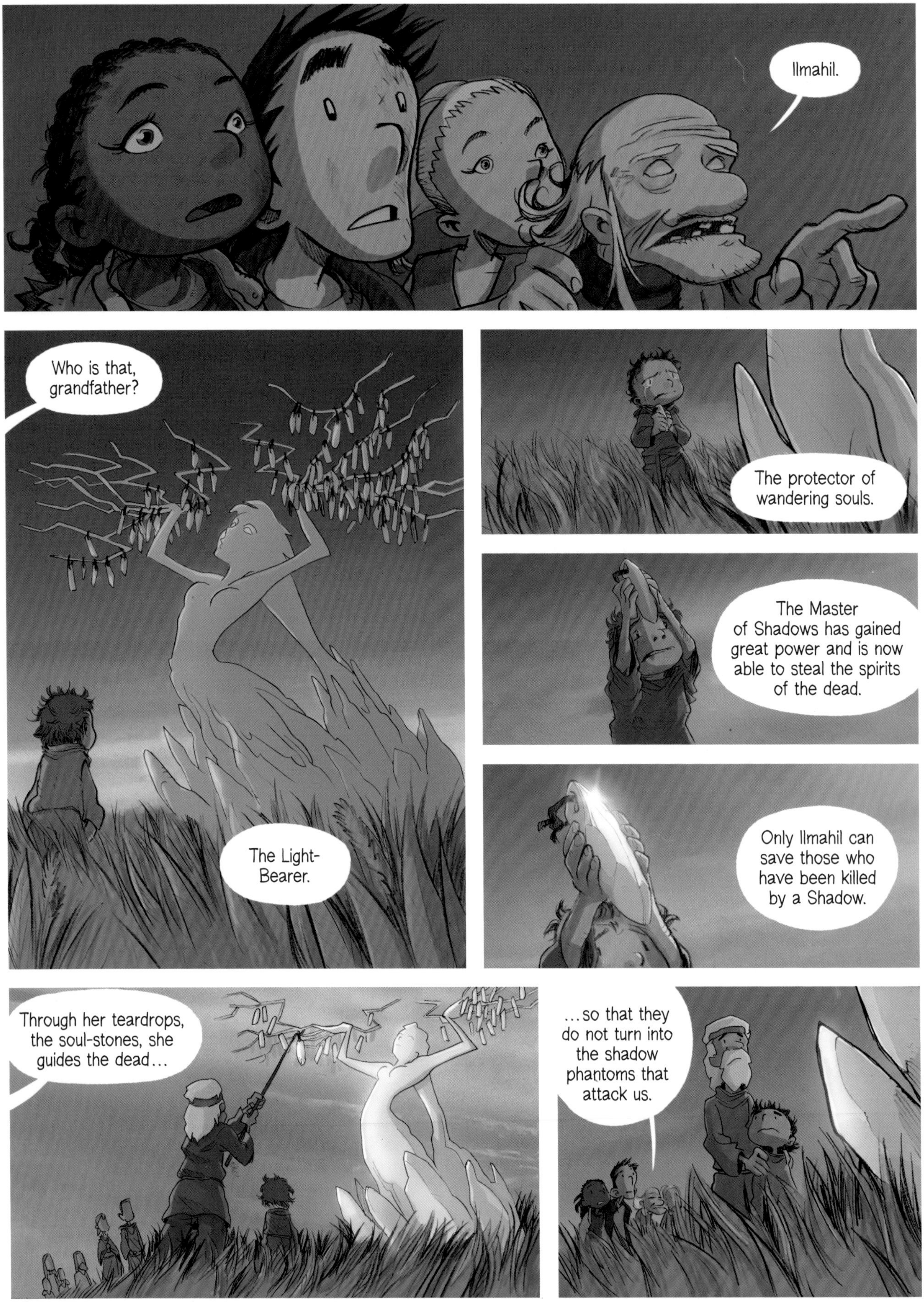

Ilmahil.
Who is that, grandfather?
The Light-Bearer.
The protector of wandering souls.
The Master of Shadows has gained great power and is now able to steal the spirits of the dead.
Only Ilmahil can save those who have been killed by a Shadow.
Through her teardrops, the soul-stones, she guides the dead...
...so that they do not turn into the shadow phantoms that attack us.

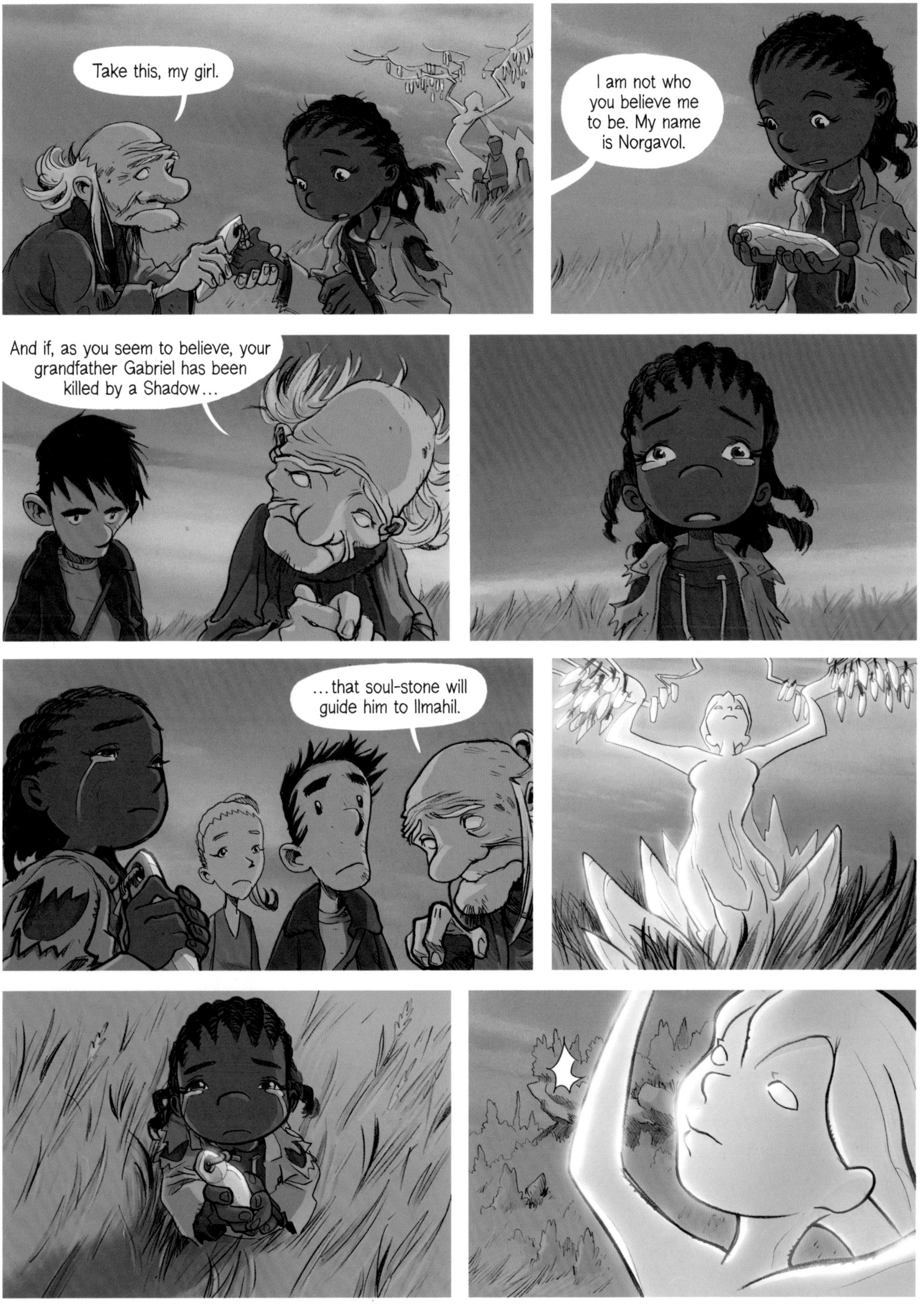
Take this, my girl.
I am not who you believe me to be. My name is Norgavol.
And if, as you seem to believe, your grandfather Gabriel has been killed by a Shadow…
…that soul-stone will guide him to Ilmahil.

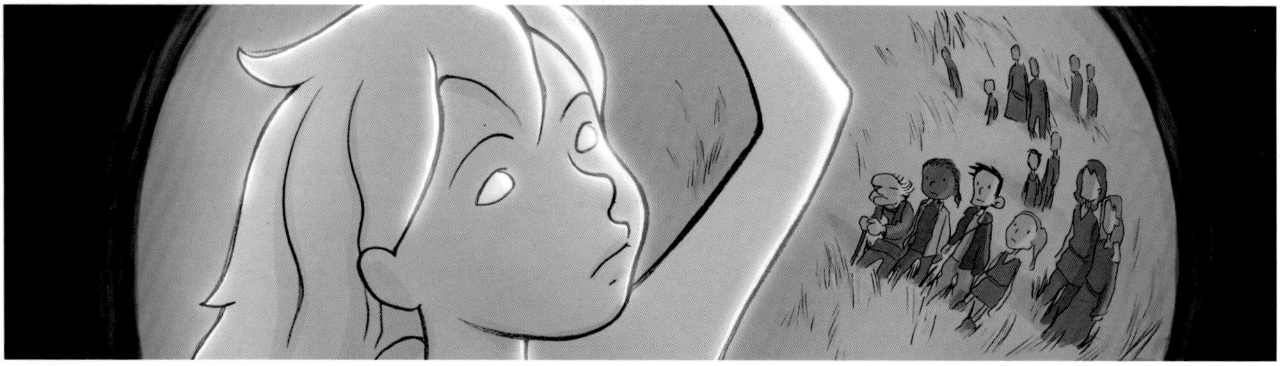

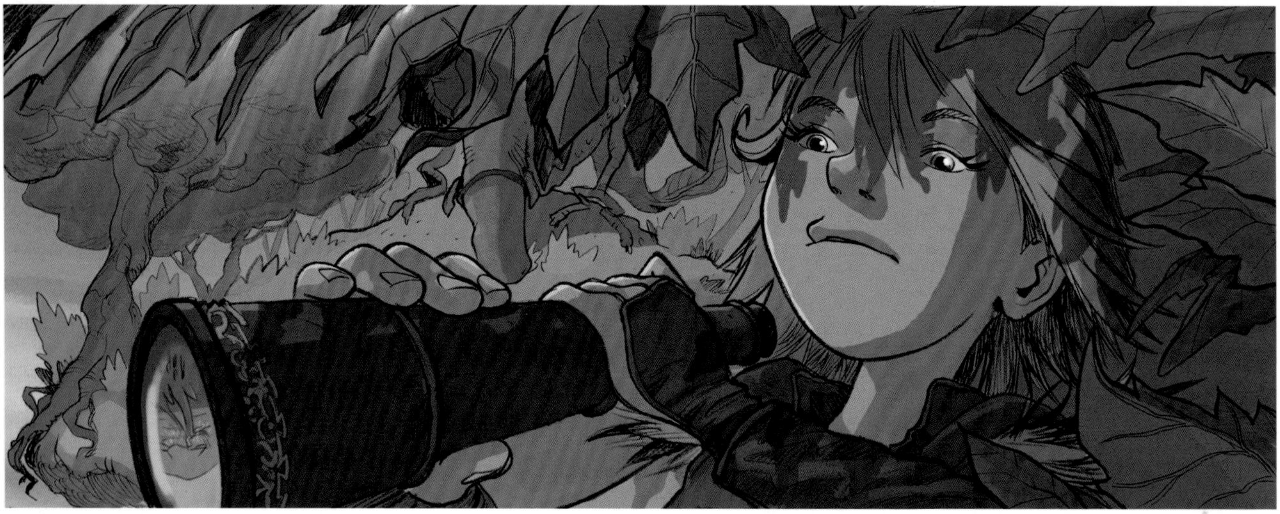

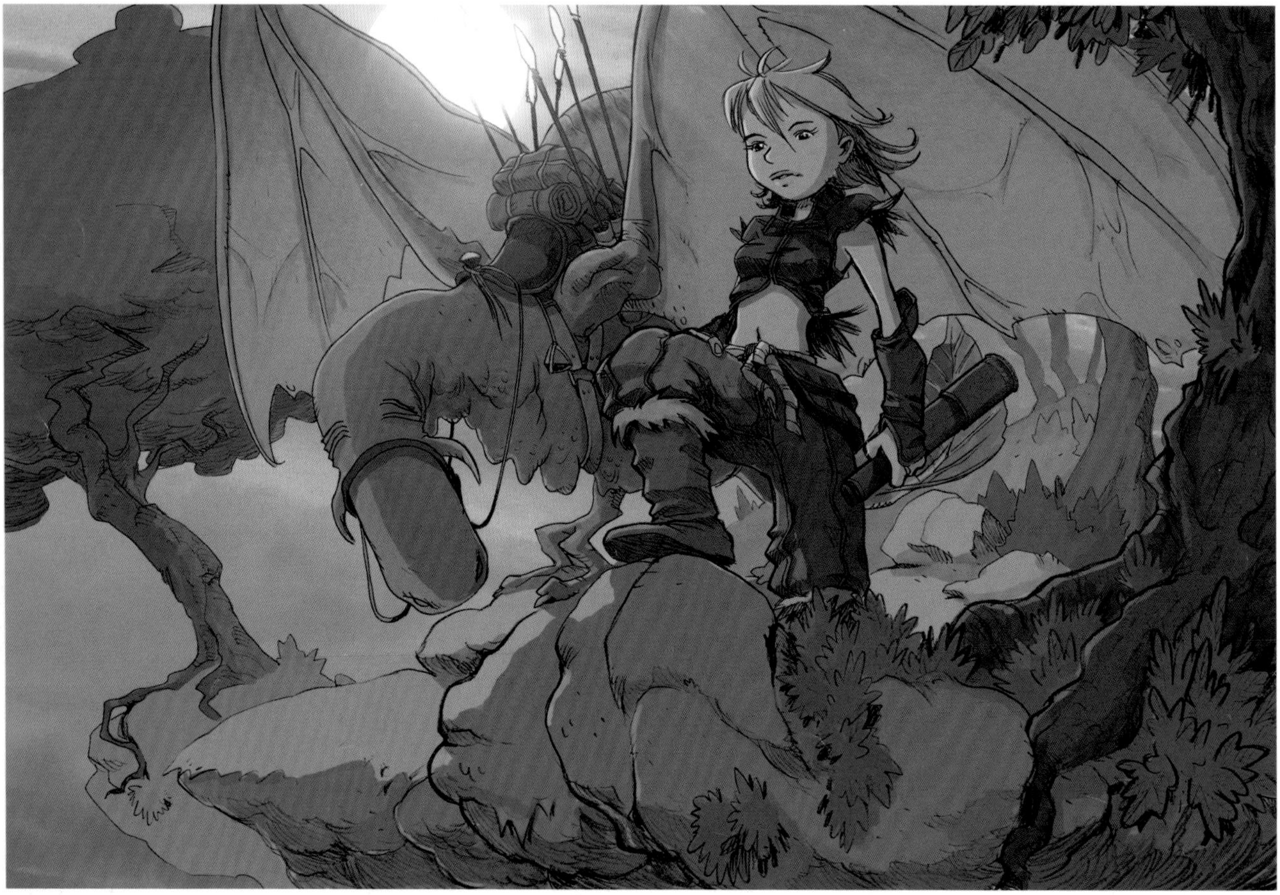

NExt Episode...

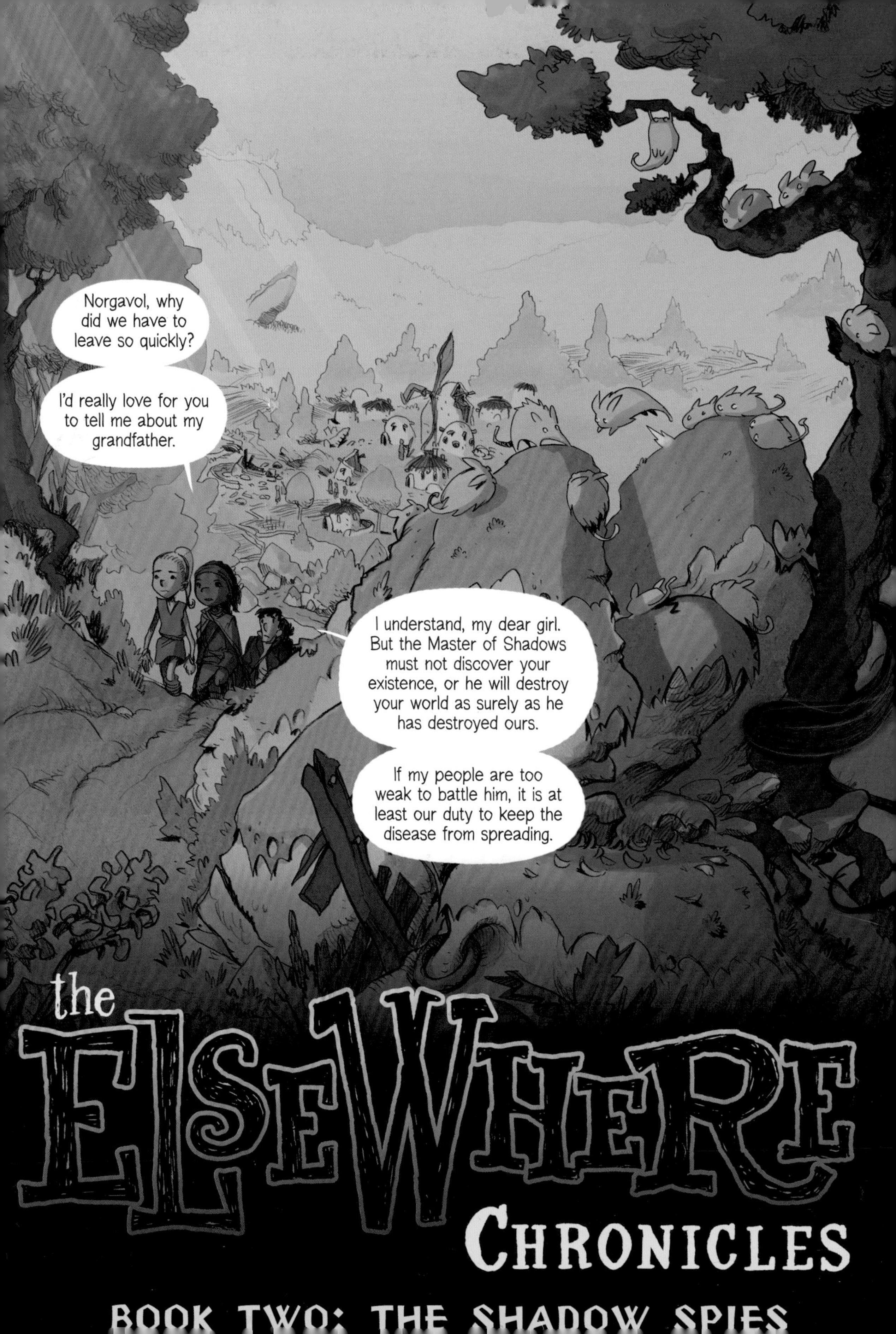
Norgavol, why did we have to leave so quickly?
I'd really love for you to tell me about my grandfather.
I understand, my dear girl. But the Master of Shadows must not discover your existence, or he will destroy your world as surely as he has destroyed ours.
If my people are too weak to battle him, it is at least our duty to keep the disease from spreading.
the ELSEWHERE CHRONICLES
BOOK TWO: THE SHADOW SPIES

Art by Bannister
Story by Nykko
Colors by Jaffré
Translation by Carol Klio Burrell

First American edition published in 2009 by Graphic Universe™.
Published by arrangement with S.A. DUPUIS, Belgium.

Graphic Universe™
A division of Lerner Publishing Group, Inc.
241 First Avenue North
Minneapolis, MN 55401 U.S.A.

Website address: www.lernerbooks.com

Library of Congress Cataloging-in-Publication Data

Bannister. [Passage. English]
The shadow door / art by Bannister ; story by Nykko ; [colors by Jaffré ;
translation by Carol Klio Burrell]. — 1st American ed.
p.   cm. — (The ElseWhere chronicles ; bk. 1)
Summary: Four friends discover a movie projector that opens a passageway into
a world threatened by creatures of shadow, where their only weapon is light.
ISBN: 978-0-7613-4459-9 (lib. bdg. : alk. paper)
1. Graphic novels. [1. Graphic novels. 2. Horror stories.] I. Nykko. II. Jaffré.
III. Burrell, Carol Klio. IV. Title.
PZ7.7.B34Sh 2009
741.5'973—dc22   2008039442

Manufactured in the United States of America
1 2 3 4 5 6 - BP - 14 13 12 11 10 09

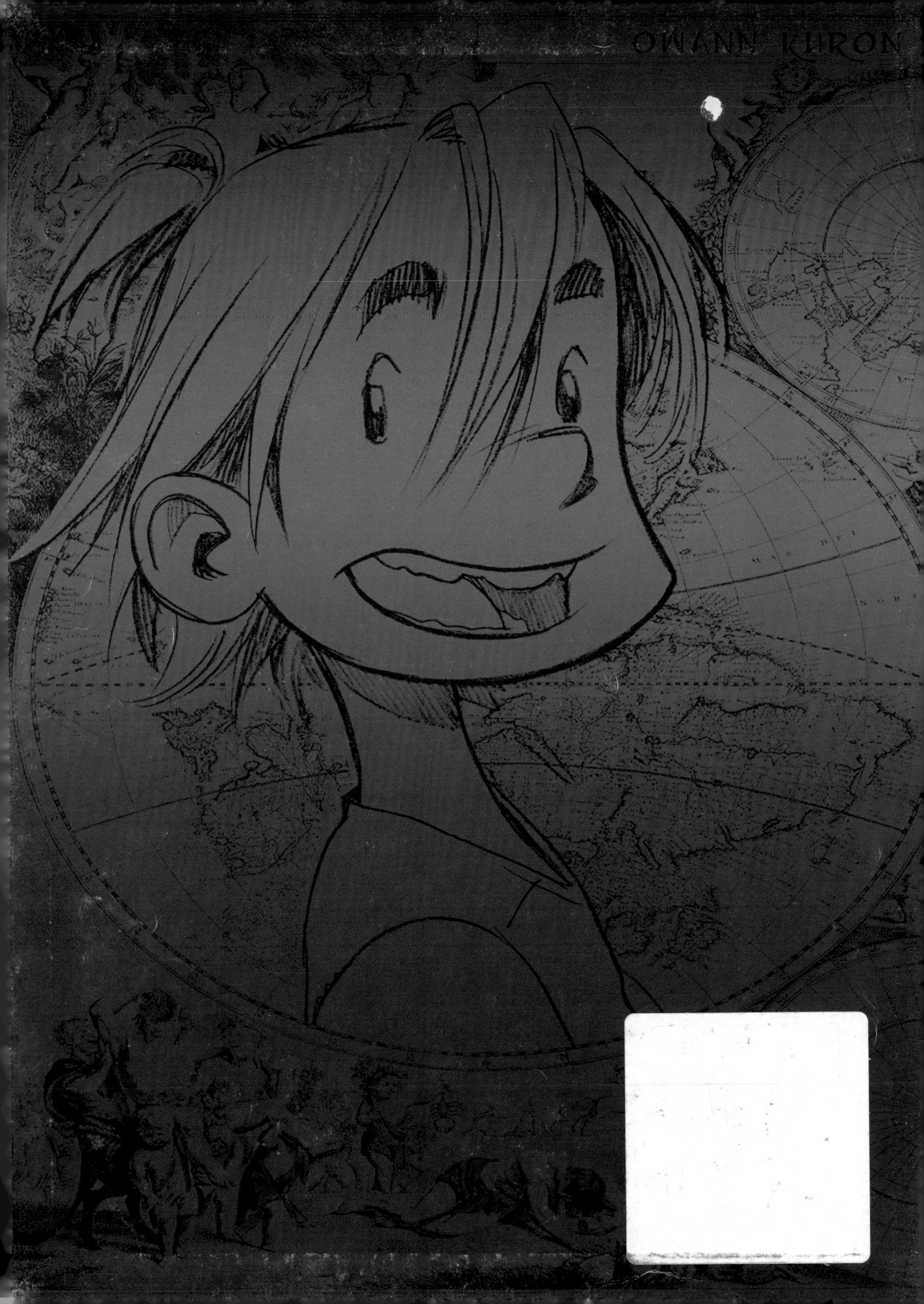
OWANN KURON